. . . and those who fear life are already three parts dead.

—Bertrand Russell

. . . and I guess it isn't too important now that they all die. I will be satisfied to make them three parts dead.

—Mack Bolan, THE EXECUTIONER

THE EXECUTIONER:

Battle Mask

by
Don Pendleton

PINNACLE BOOKS • LOS ANGELES

THE EXECUTIONER: BATTLE MASK

An original Pinnacle Books edition,
published for the first time anywhere.

ISBN: 0-523-40301-1

First printing, April 1970
Second printing, October 1970
Third printing, December 1970
Fourth printing, June 1971
Fifth printing, December 1971
Sixth printing, June 1972
Seventh printing, July 1972
Eighth printing, November 1972
Ninth printing, March 1974
Tenth printing, May 1975
Eleventh printing, December 1976
Twelfth printing, October 1977
Thirteenth printing, April 1978
Fourteenth printing, June 1978
Fifteenth printing, December 1978

PINNACLE BOOKS, INC.
2029 Century Park East
Los Angeles, California 90067

PROLOGUE

The priest who christened Mack Bolan did not, as some of his former army acquaintances claim, sprinkle the infant with human blood. His "executions" in the jungles and hamlets of Vietnam were not, as some leftist correspondents claimed, the acts of a cold-blooded murderer who was being sponsored by the U.S. government. Boland *was* a professional soldier, a career man with ten years of unblemished service behind him when he was consigned to the weird warfare being staged in Southeast Asia. He exemplified what the army psychologist called "the perfect sniper—a man who can kill personally yet impersonally, and who can objectively accept the blood on his hands as a matter of national duty, not just personal conscience . . ."

Sgt. Bolan was an expert marksman and a disciplined soldier. He could command himself, and he could command others. As his reputation grew during the two years in Vietnam, he became known as "the Executioner." He was feared by the enemy, admired by his superiors, and held slightly in awe by his associates. The verified accounting of Bolan's "kills" in Vietnam shows 32 high-ranking North Vietnamese officers, 46 VC guerrilla leaders, and 17 VC village officials.

Bolan was philosophic about his army specialty. "Someone had to do it," he once remarked. "I can do it." At the age of 30, and after two full years of combat duty, the nerveless perfectionist was called home to bury the victims of another brand of warfare—his mother, father, and teenage sister. For

1

the police, it was an open and shut case of suicide and double murder—with the father taking the blame. Bolan saw it somewhat differently, learning that his father had been harassed, brutalized, and pushed beyond the limits of human endurance by a loan-sharking operation which was controlled by an international crime syndicate, popularly called "the Mafia."

Convinced that the police were powerless to act in the tragedy, Executioner Bolan turned his sharpshooter's sights onto the guilty ones and launched "the most impossible war in history." He became an over-night American legend, one lone man versus the seemingly invincible forces of the dreaded Mafia. The Executioner brought Vietnam tactics to the jungles of the American underworld and, in a vicious and bloody battle that staggered and stupefied the opposition, virtually neutralized the Mafia's influence in Bolan's home town.

In the aftermath of the Pittsfield War, prognosticators were quoting million-to-one odds against an old age for Mack Bolan. The object of the most massive police manhunt in modern history and with a $100,000 Mafia pricetag on his head, the plucky fighter moved his thunder and lightning to Los Angeles, recruited a "death squad" of former Vietnam buddies, and took on the powerful "family" of L.A. czar Julian DiGeorge. Though harassed by the unrelenting efforts of the Los Angeles police, Bolan and his "hellish squad" succeeded in crippling the DiGeorge operations in Southern California. The victory was a hollow one for Bolan, however; his own casualties were 100% and DiGeorge himself escaped the final showdown at the Mafia stronghold near Balboa, a California resort town.

The odds against Bolan again pyramided.

Alone, wounded, sought by the police and by every ambitious hoodlum in the country, it seemed that the Executioner was due for extermination. For Mack Bolan, however, life was a road which stretched between birth and death; he had not yet conceded that last bloody mile.

Chapter One

FLUSHED

Mack Bolan was dreaming, and he knew it, and he liked the dream, and he was becoming increasingly irritated with the demands that he awaken. In the dream, his former comrades of the Death Squad were with him once again, and they were sprawled about the large living room of the beach house base-camp.

Chopper Fontenelli and Deadeye Washington were wisecracking about the status of black men in the Mafia brotherhood. Flower Child Andromede was reciting gruesome poetry to Gunsmoke Harrington while Harrington practiced his quick-draw. Boom-boom Hoffower was boobytrapping a light fixture while Bloodbrother Loudelk quietly kibitzed the operation with Indian signs. Whispering Zitka was throwing a stiletto at flies- while Politician Blancanales and Gadgets Schwartz were fiddling with an electronic panel.

The panel was causing Bolan's irritation. It persisted in emitting loud squawks, endangering the rosy dream. It was nice having the hellish bunch together again. Suddenly, the irritation was gone and Bolan was wide awake. He was alone in the dimly lighted room, fully dressed, half reclining in a large lounger. The security monitor, a makeshift console occupying a low table to Bolan's right, was flashing an amber light and buzzing furiously.

Bolan was on his feet and gliding across the room toward a window even before his conscious mind could fully assess the situation. He pulled back a drape and peered into the blackness, then

5

hastened back to the monitor to check the location-identifier. The flashing light indicated an intruder at the gateway to the drive, some 200 yards from the house. Abruptly another light began flashing, then another. Bolan suspended a machine-pistol from his shoulder, smiled grimly, and moved soundlessly onto the side patio. The house occupied an isolated stretch of beach on California's rugged southern coastline just above Santa Monica, sheltered between sheer cliffs to each side, with the surging ocean to the rear. Bolan had selected the place because of the remoteness and natural defensibility; it had seemed a perfect base camp for his Death Squad in their operations against the Mafia. Now, however, there was no squad. Only Bolan remained, and he was wondering if the place might not turn out to be an inescapable trap for a lone defender. The isolation bore in on him, emphasized by the muted roar of the ocean behind him and the cloud-darkened skies above. And someone was coming calling.

Bolan hurried back into the house and picked up a waiting suitcase, carried it outside and across the patio, and tossed it onto the seat of a black sedan. He started the engine, left it idling quietly, and went back to the forward wall of the patio. There he lined up a collection of flare-shells, checked the azimuth and scale settings of a small cannon-like object, and immediately dropped in a shell. The tube belched a puff of smoke and gave out a soft *whump*. Bolan quickly re-set the azimuth and dropped in another shell, and was lifting binoculars to his eyes even before the second firing occurred.

The first shell exploded high in the air directly above the gateway and the second one opened at the midway point. Two automobiles had been moving slowly along the drive, without lights. Each halted abruptly, in reaction to the sudden dazzling brilliance of the flares. A door on the lead vehicle was flung open and two men erupted into the open.

Bolan caught a familiar face in the vision field of his binoculars. He grunted in recognition of Lou Pena, one of the local Mafia "enforcers." So, he calmly realized, the Family had finally tracked him down. He shushed the butterflies in his stomach and reached for his long-distance sniper, fitted his eye to the high-power scope, and picked up a target from among the rapidly dispersing invaders. His hand squeezed into the trigger guard, the big piece roared and slammed against his shoulder, and his target abruptly disappeared from the vision-field. He swung the long Mauser toward the vehicles and rapid-fired the entire clip into the enemy's mobile units. The lead car exploded into spectacular flames which quickly spread to the car behind. Someone began shouting loud instructions and a volley of returning gunfire swept into the beach house.

Bolan grinned, dropped the Mauser, and ran to the far end of the wall, where Fontenelli's prized fifty-calibre watercooled machine gun was emplaced. He hurriedly checked the ammo belt, positioned the swing-stops to a 30-degree sweep, and affixed the continuous-fire mechanism he had devised only hours earlier.

The heavy staccato of the big fifty began lacing the air, the muzzle swinging freely between the stops under the impetus of its own eruptions. Satisfied that the device was operating properly, Bolan sprinted for his car, climbed behind the far wheel, and gunned out across the parking lot in a spray of gravel.

He hit the driveway with lights out and in

whining traction. Just as he entered the periphery of flare-light, an object loomed up over his front bumper. He felt the impact even as he recognized the object as a human figure and saw it hurling off into the darkness. And then he was in full light, hunched low over the steering wheel and in screaming acceleration. His head was jerked involuntarily as a projectile crashed through his windshield. Something tore into the seat alongside his shoulder. He was aware of excitedly running figures to either side of him and projectiles were now zinging into the body of the car from all sides. He put out a mental forcefield of protection around his tires, gas tank, and engine, and swung wide around the blazing wrecks that blocked the drive. One of his rear wheels dug deeply into the sandy softness at the driveway's edge, throwing the vehicle into a heart-stopping swerve. He spun the wheel into the skid, regained control, and swung back onto the hard surface of the drive at full acceleration. The tires screeched in protest, but held on, and dug in, and then he was rolling free and angling into the road.

Scattered shots were still sounding behind him. He glanced back over his shoulder as he gained the roadway. Several men were running along the drive. He thought he detected the gleam of metal, reflecting the now-dying glow of the flares, on the road behind him. He hoped it was not another vehicle, but decided that it probably was just that. As he topped the rise that would drop him onto the main highway, the headlamps of an automobile flared up in his rear-vision mirror. Yes, they had another vehicle. Bolan forced himself to unwind a bit and to slow for the approach to the highway. He debated furiously for a micro-second as to which direction to take, immediately made up his mind, and swept into the northbound lane.

8

According to the roadmap which he'd burned into his brain, he would intersect a back road several miles up, to carry him easterly into the interior. He wondered if Braddock's Hardcase police detail was still in operation and, if so, how long it would take them to react to this latest sure-clue to Mack Bolan's whereabouts. Assuming, of course, that someone had heard and reported the disturbance. He pulled a quick traffic check of the highway and decided that easily a dozen cars could have passed within earshot of the gunfire. Bolan shrugged his shoulders and leaned into sweeping curve. Behind him, headlights were turning onto the highway, coming his way. Hell . . . it didn't make much difference, did it? Cops or *Mafiosi*, what was the difference? Either one spelled out the same effect for Mack Bolan. He carefully removed the sling of the machine pistol and placed the wicked little weapon on the seat beside his leg. He glanced into the back seat, noting the presence of the heavy suitcase. The money bag . . . or what was left of it. And what was left of Mack Bolan? That was it, wasn't it. A bullet-riddled car, perhaps even now spewing a trail of gasoline from a punctured tank. A machine pistol with five clips of ammo. A bag of money. Yes, that was it. *No, he decided suddenly . . . there was more than that.* There were the ghosts of seven dead good men, and then there were the spirits of two more who might spend the rest of their lives behind bars. There was Bolan's utter disgust and cold hatred for anything *Mafia.* There were the brains of a very professional soldier, and the determination to win this lousy war.

Bolan squared his shoulders, loosened his grip on the steering wheel, and let his eyes range ahead to search for the appearance of that back road. He knew now where he was headed—knew where he had to go and what he had to do. He had known it back there with the decision to swing north. It was an idea he'd toyed with since the first battle, at Pittsfield. And now he had finally made the decision. The decision to *live*, and to once again take the battle to the *Mafiosi*. To *live*, Bolan must rid himself of his greatest liability. His *face*. And Bolan knew a man with a gift for faces. He'd watched Jim Brantzen reconstruct many battle-torn faces, and Brantzen now had his own clinic in Palm Village, not a hundred crow-flying miles from Bolan's present location. The problem, Bolan recognized, was that he was not a crow. That hundred miles could seem like a thousand, especially if the cops got into the act. He stiffened suddenly, spotting the dimly marked junction ahead, and swerved onto the narrow backroad without slowing his speed.

Mack Bolan, the Executioner, had been flushed toward a new horizon. He just hoped that he would be able to find it before the world rolled over and crushed him. Headlights turned in, far behind him. He floorboarded the gas pedal and searched him memory for the route ahead. All of life he could claim lay ahead of him. And, perhaps, only death.

Chapter Two

FLIGHT

Julian (Deej) DiGeorge paced the small study of his Palm Springs retreat, frequently eyeing the telephone and glancing at his watch. He stepped to a shuttered window and peered through a slit. The backs of two of his best boys hove into view, then moved out of sight as they restlessly moved about the grounds. Deej grunted with satisfaction and turned once more to the telephone. Why didn't the damn thing ring? Lou should have made the hit by now and be bursting to pass along the good news. Deej could not, he knew, count Bolan out until that telephone sounded. The nervy punk was just too full of . . . DiGeorge shivered involuntarily and went back to the window. It had been a long time since Deej DiGeorge, boss of the Western Mafia, had been frightened of another human being. He was frightened now, and he admitted it . . . to himself. Sure, sure he was scared. It'd take an idiot to not be scared, with a maniac like that Bolan running around loose.

His eyes swung in near-panic as the knob of the study door turned, then knuckles sounded lightly on the panel. DiGeorge detoured by way of his desk, scooped up a nickel-plated revolver, and went quietly to the door. "Yeh?" he asked.

A faintly amused feminine voice said, "Poppa, what are you doing in there behind locked doors? Making love to the housekeeper?"

DiGeorge turned the lock and opened the door. Andrea DiGeorge, a striking brunette with long shiny hair worn in a fold-singer free-fall, pushed

11

provocatively encased hips into the study, eyed the revolver in her father's fist and laughed softly. "Careful," she said, "the bogeyman'll get you."

"Not as long as I got Charles Henry, here," DiGeorge replied soberly, shaking the pistol.

The girl pouted her lips and said, "Yeah, old Charlie there is a formidable weapon . . . on a pistol range. I'll bet he's never thrown down on a living thing, though. Seriously, Poppa, why don't you . . ."

The telephone sounded, and Andrea immediately lost her audience. DiGeorge's eyes flared in a delighted reaction. He all but leapt onto the telephone, leaving his daughter standing open-mouthed in the doorway. He snatched up the instrument and breathlessly said, "Yeah?"

"That you, Deej?" Lou Pena's mournful tones inquired.

"Well who'n hell you think it would . . ." DiGeorge caught his breath and flicked a glance at the doorway. Andrea had departed. He sank limply onto the corner of the desk. There was no mistaking the failure in Pena's voice. "All right, Lou," DiGeorge said. "How'd it go?"

There was a brief silence from the other end of the connection. DiGeorge could almost see the wheels of Pena's brain whirling toward the right words. "I . . . he got away from us, Deej," he said dismally.

"Whattya mean, he *got away?*" DiGeorge shrilled.

"I mean he got away. Julio and some boys took off after him, but he had a pretty good lead. I don't know."

"You don't know *what?*"

"Well, I dunno if they'll be able to catch him or not. He had a pretty good lead, and in a good car.

Uh ... Ralph Scarpetti's dead. So's Al Reggnio. And two or three others are hurt, not seriously. I got a nick myself."

DiGeorge swore softly into the transmitter, then carefully placed the revolver on the desk.

"And he burned up two of our cars. That's how come I'm so long checking in. Had to send a boy in after some transportation."

DiGeorge's eyes were glazing. He loosened his collar and rocked gently to and fro on the edge of the desk. Presently he said, "So. Some hit, eh? I send fifteen boys out after one lousy punk and I wind up with two dead, half a dozen hurt, two cars . . ." DiGeorge's voice choked off. He tugged at his collar again.

"Listen, Deej, this guy is no punk," Pena offered defensively. "He's a damn one-man army. God, he shot these flares up in the air, see, and caught us right out in the open. Hell, I can't figure how he even knew we were coming. It was pitch-dark, and we weren't making any noise, not even breathing hard. Then, out of nowhere, *bloom*, here's these goddam flares floating down on us. And he opens up with a goddam heavy machine gun. Hell, we're lucky any of us are alive to talk about it. This guy ain't no punk, Deej."

"Yeah. Okay, Lou. Where are you now?"

"Pay phone, north side of Santa Monica. I guess we got out of there just in time. Met a sheriff's car on the way back, lights flashing and all that crap. I guess somebody . . ."

"Stop guessing, Lou, and bring what's left of your boys on out here."

"Well . . . listen . . ."

DiGeorge sighed. "Yeah?"

"I already started things rolling. I got ahold of Patty. He's spreading people all up and down the damn highways. I told him to cover everything,

13

and solid. Gas stations, bus stations, road junctions, the whole bit. I told him, uh, I hope this's okay, Deej, I told him to hell with the expense, the sky's the limit. We just want to get Bolan. Right?"

DiGeorge sighed again. "Right, Lou, that's exactly right. But you come on back here. I want to start mapping out a foolproof campaign. I don't want any more half-assing around."

"Okay ... uh ... I'm sorry as hell, Deej."

DiGeorge quietly hung up the telephone, stared at it dolefully for a long moment, then said, "You sure are, Lou baby."

Bolan sent his car powering into a squealing turn to follow the torturous mountain road, crested the hill, and began to drop into the interior valley. The twinkling lights of a small town were showing, far ahead. He glanced at his watch and decided that he was making pretty good time, even with all his zig-zagging and backtracking through the mountains. His gasoline supply was getting low; the powerful car could consume a lot of fuel during two hours of this type of driving. The lights in the distance should be Palm Village, he decided. He wondered if he had gas enough to make it on in, and whether or not he would come onto a service station on this lonely road. A dull ache in his right ankle told him that the injury from the Balboa battle was again demanding attention. He felt shelled-out, weary, and entirely resigned to the role fate had decreed for him. He was going to die by the gun, he knew this. The only question remaining unanswered, in Bolan's mind, was the *when* of it. *Why not right now,* he mused. Why prolong it? A forlorn pride surged up from the depths of his weariness. He knew, of course, why it had to be prolonged. A man did not choose a time and place to die; he chose a battleground for life. Bolan had chosen his own battleground. The rest of it was simply a matter of fighting the battle to the best of his ability, and all the way to the end. Was that a philosophy, or a resignation? Bolan shook his head. He recognized it as neither. Philosophies, to Bolan's mind, were no more than idle games. In the final analysis, a man either spent his life or bargained it away. Bolan was spending his.

He then swept around another curve and immediately began slowing for a brightly lighted intersection straight ahead. A roadside sign with GAS-OIL-CAFE caught his attention. It directed him to a rundown building with a single gas pump, occupying one corner of the road junction. Bolan eased on the brakes and swung onto a dusty ramp, bringing the car to a halt at the gas pump. He opened the door and stepped out, gingerly testing the sore ankle. Two other vehicles were parked in the shadow of the building; another was angled toward the highway at the far end of the ramp. Limping slightly, he went around the rear of his car and entered the building. Shelves on the back wall contained a dreary assortment of dry groceries. An ancient pinball machine occupied a dark corner. A rough-hewn counter with four stools constituted the "cafe." Behind the dingy counter stood a middle-aged woman in a grease-spotted white apron. Two of the stools were being held down by a pair of elderly men. They wore soiled work clothes, were drinking beer from cans, and they were staring interestedly at Bolan. When he smiled at them, they turned away. Bolan moved on to the end of the counter and addressed the woman. "I need some gas," he told her.

"You'll have to pump it yourself," she replied, in a surprisingly cultured voice.

"All right," he said agreeably. "I'll have some coffee, too."

She shook her head. "Sorry, I'm out of coffee. How about a beer?"

Bolan grinned and declined with a shake of his head. He stepped toward the door.

"Don't go out there, son," said a voice behind him.

Bolan paused with a hand on the door and gazed over his shoulder. One of the men at the counter had swivelled about and was regarding him with an intent stare. "I said, don't go out there," the old man repeated.

"Why not?" Bolan inquired, his hackles already rising.

"That car still out there? Edge o' the road?"

Bolan nodded his head and moved casually away from the door.

"Three men in it," the man informed him. "They was in here askin' about you, little while ago. Figger they're sittin' out there just waitin' for you now."

"How do you know they were asking about *me?*" Bolan said.

The old man's eyes raked Bolan from end to end. "Described you pretty well," he replied. "And they're packin' guns."

"How do you know that?"

"Same way I know you got one under that jacket there. They got a shotgun, too. Saw it'n their front seat when they drove up. Don't act like cops, either."

"They're not," Bolan assured him. He turned to the door again.

"My old pickup's out back," the man said, in a tense voice.

"Yeah?" Bolan was trying to appear relaxed and nonchalant as his eyes probed the vehicle at the intersection.

"If you was to leave your car sittin' there, I could probably drive you right past 'em."

Bolan examined the offer.

"I was 'bout ready to go, anyway," the man added.

"There's a suitcase on my back seat," Bolan murmured. "I have to have it."

The old man sild off the stool. "I'll go out and raise your hood and stick the hose in the gas tank," he said. "They'll think you're gettin' serviced. Can I get in that car from this side?"

Bolan was gauging the angle of vision between the two cars. If the *Mafiosi* remained in their vehicle, they would not be able to see between Bolan's car and the building, especially with Bolan's hood elevated. "I'll get the bag out and meet you in the rear," he suggested.

The old man nodded as he shuffled past Bolan and out the door. Moments later the hood of Bolan's car sprang open, blocking Bolan's view of the other vehicle. He quickly stepped outside, leaned into his car for the suitcase, then moved quickly around the corner of the small structure. A rattle-trap pickup truck sat on a dirt driveway at the rear. Bolan quietly deposited his luggage in the bed of the truck and climbed into the cab. He sat on the floorboards and eased the pistol into the ready position. He had hardly become settled when his elderly benefactor climbed in on the driver's side and, without a word, cranked the engine. They jounced around the far end of the building and pulled slowly onto the highway, coming to a full stop directly opposite the stake-out vehicle. Bolan saw the old man nod genially

17

at the *Mafiosi*, then the gears ground and they lurched on through the intersection.

"They barely gave me a look-see," the old man reported, chuckling. "Too busy tryin' to see you gettin' back in your car."

Bolan counted to ten, then lifted himself into the seat. The highway junction was disappearing around a gentle curve, and again the road was heading into a steep descent. "Better get all the speed you can out of this bucket, sir," he advised. "Those guys won't sit there and stare at an empty car forever."

"Ain't had so much fun since Anzio," the oldster declared. "You figger they'll come shootin' when they find out we suckered 'em?"

"That's what I figger," Bolan replied quietly. "You'll have to drop me at the first convenient spot. If they ever catch up with you, tell them I was holding a gun on you."

"Shoot! I ain't never turned tail on vermin before. And, believe me, son, them back there is *vermin*." The old man wiped his lips with the back of his hand. "It's ten miles into Palm Village," he added. "I guess I can get you that far. That's where I'm headed anyway."

Bolan produced his wallet, extracted two fifties, and shoved them into the man's shirt pocket.

"You don't have to do that."

Bolan smiled grimly. "I couldn't possibly do enough," he said. "You have a right to know ... those *vermin* back there are Mafia liquidators."

The old man smiled. "Shoot, I know that. Know you, too. Seen nothing but your picture on teevee for most a week now."

Bolan shot a glance through the rear window, grunted deep in his throat, and observed, "So ... I guess you know what you're doing."

The man's head snapped in a decisive nod.

18

"Sure do. Know what you're doing, too. Want you to know, you got most of the people behind you. You're a national hero . . . know that?"

Bolan grinned again. He lightly massaged the grip of his pistol and swivelled sideways in the seat for a clear view to the rear. "You'd better get this vehicle moving faster than this," he said worriedly.

"She's gulpin' all the gas she can handle. Like me, she ain't exactly in her prime."

Bolan peered despairingly at the speedometer. They had not even achieved the speed of flight. He threw off the safety of his pistol and began searching the road ahead for a place to fight. The Executioner's flight appeared to be drawing to a close.

Chapter Three

THE HORIZON

It was shortly past midnight when the ancient Ford pickup rolled to an indecisive halt at the junction of a country lane, just west of Palm Village. The tall figure descending from the passenger's side of the cab dragged a suitcase from the bed of the truck, then stepped clear and threw a silent salute to the driver. A darkly weathered face smiled back at him, and the old vehicle chugged away.

Limping slightly, Bolan headed down the tree-arched lane into inky darkness. He halted about ten yards from the intersection, moved behind a tree, and sat quietly on the up-ended suitcase, patiently waiting.

Moments later another vehicle came to a halt in the intersection, then eased onto the shoulder of the main road. The headlights were quickly extinguished. A car door opened and gently closed, then another. A muffled voice declared: "Yeah, he stopped here, all right. We'll check it out. You stay on th' truck." The smooth acceleration of a powerful engine signalled the departure of the second vehicle.

Bolan arose with a quiet sigh, clipped a pencil flashlight to a low-hanging tree-branch, turned the tiny flashlight on, carefully positioned the suitcase, then moved swiftly and silently behind the line of trees and toward the intersection. Two men were moving cautiously toward him, one to either side of the lane. He sensed, rather than saw or heard, their approach, freezing behind a large elm and allowing them to pass. The men had obviously spotted the faint flow of the pencil-flash and were closing on it with great care.

Their quarry smiled grimly as his stalkers moved downrange between him and the light, their shadowy forms taking on bulky substance against the lighter background. He stepped soundlessly onto the pavement and tagged along, bringing up the rear in the apex position of the three-man triangle. The two were perfectly outlined now as they moved on in a half-crouch, pistols thrust forward and ready.

One of the men made an excited sound as the shadowy form of the grounded suitcase loomed up beyond the light. Both pistols exploded into sound and flame, and the suitcase toppled over onto its side with an ominous thud.

"Hold it, hold it!" an excited voice commanded. "We got 'im!"

"Then why's the damn light . . ."

"Turn around," suggested a calm baritone behind them.

The men whirled as one, weapons roaring again even with no target in sight. A stuttering chatter overrode the other sounds, and extinguished them. A pained voice exclaimed, "Oh God, Frankie . . . oh God!" Bolan's weapon stuttered again, very briefly. He stepped forward, gingerly probed the bodies with an extended foot, and said "uh-huh" with evident satisfaction.

Bolan wasted no time over the dead. He retrieved the pencil-flash and the suitcase and returned quickly to the junction of the main road. There he concealed himself behind a small bushy growth and began another quiet wait. He lit a cigarette and calmly dragged on it, filling his lungs and holding the smoke for several seconds, then exhaling in short bursts of calculatingly released tensions. On the third inhalation, the eastern horizon began glowing with the suggestion of approaching headlights. Bolan carefully crushed the cigarette beneath his foot and examined his weapon.

Moments later a speeding westbound automobile braked into the junction with a squeal of tires, hunching to a halt just inside the lane and slightly downrange from Bolan's position. With engine idling and headlamps in full glare along the overshadowed lane, the driver of the vehicle stepped onto the roadway and called out softly, "Frank? Cholli? Be careful! He wasn't in th' truck!"

Bolan had moved onto the lane and was approaching the vehicle from the rear. "Wonder where he could be?" he whispered harshly.

The man said, "I dunno, he ..." He stiffened suddenly, reaching into the car and trying to swing toward Bolan with the same motion. The stock of a sawed-off shotgun became entangled in the steering wheel. Grotesquely off balance and fighting frantically to free the shotgun, the man screeched: "No, Bolan, wait! I give ..."

What he planned to give was lost in the explosive bark of a single report from Bolan's weapon. The bullet punched through an upflung hand and crunched into the bone between the eyes. The man crumbled, his limp body sagging onto the door, then flopping to the asphalt below. Bolan rolled him clear, dropped the shotgun across the body, and stepped into the car. He backed to the intersection, picked up his suitcase and threw it into the rear seat, then swung onto the main road and proceeded easterly toward Palm Village.

Entering the residential outskirts of the city some moments later, Bolan came upon the battered pickup truck in which he had recently been a passenger. It was now even more battered, having apparently veered off the road, climbed the curbing, and come to rest against a tree. A human form lay on the grass beside the wrecked vehicle. A police cruiser was parked nearby and a uniformed officer stood at the edge of the road, excitedly waving Bolan on through with a flashlight, though there were no other vehicles on the road. Slowing through a gathering crowd of curious, nightclothed people, Bolan overheard a man exclaim: "Why, it's old Harry Thompson!"

Another voice observed, "Someone's taken a shotgun to 'im."

A hot rage clutching at his chest, Bolan halted alongside the policeman. Careful to keep his face in shadow, he said tightly, "Anybody hurt?"

The young officer then nodded his head in exasperation and said, "Please, keep moving. We gotta keep this road open for the ambulance."

"Still alive, then?"

"I think so. Move along, will you? I can't let this road get jammed up!"

"There was some shooting about a mile back," Bolan said, his tone chatty. "Might be some connection to this."

"We'll check it out," the officer assured him. "Will you please move ..."

Bolan applied pressure to the accelerator and left the scene quickly behind. His fingers were white on the steering wheel, the only outward sign of his inner raging. His anger was directed mostly toward himself; he'd had no right to involve the old man in his war. Sorrow was a luxury Mack Bolan could not afford. He cleared his mind of the old man, directed the car on to the business district, and abandoned it in a darkened public parking lot. Setting off on foot for the eastern edge of the city, he frequently shifted the suitcase from one hand to the other and halted occasionally to rub his swollen ankle.

It was well past midnight when he found the neat collection of modest buildings and the flower-bordered grounds of New Horizons Sanitarium. He inspected the inconspicuous sign with interest, hoping that the name would prove symbolic for him. The phrase "new horizons" was a familiar one to Bolan: Jim Brantzen had used it often enough in speaking of his surgical specialty. Brantzen himself, however, was not an easy man to read. Although he had cut through Army custom and formalities to establish a strong friendship between a commissioned officer and a non-com, there had always existed that silent barrier between the two minds. Bolan had saved Brantzen's life—not once, but twice—and there existed also that quiet bond of unspoken indebtedness. Still ... Bolan was not certain that he would be greeted here with open arms. He would be requesting an illegal operation—surgery, that is, to escape apprehension and prosecution under law—and it would be asking quite a lot of any member of a respected profession, friendships and debts notwithstanding. There was also the matter of personal hazard via the Mafia. Bolan had just been given a jolting reminder of the danger he brought into each life he touched, no matter how casually. What right had he to ...?

He stared at the neat signboard and pondered the agonizing question. Could he construct a horizon for himself upon the graves of his friends? Already seven graves lay at Bolan's feet, perhaps eight now. A distant siren sounded across the night stillness. Bolan shivered and stepped away from the New Horizon sign. Then a light flashed on outside the central building and a screen door was opened. A familiar voice said, "Well ... are you going to stand out there all night, or are you going to come in?"

Chapter Four

DESIGNS

Captain Tim Braddock, LAPD, stepped out of his car and kicked absently into the fine gravel of the parking lot as he surveyed the sprawling beach house. Carl Lyons, the young sergeant of detectives who had been with Braddock since the beginning of the Bolan Case, code-named *Hardcase*, walked around the corner of the building and approached the captain's vehicle.

"It's a sure score, Cap'n," Lyons intoned softly.

Braddock grunted and walked to the edge of the gravelled area, kneeling to inspect a deep impression left in the sand by a heavy wheel. "Would you say a semi-trailer?" he asked Lyons.

The young man knelt beside his boss and spread his hands over the wide track. "Uh huh. There's more of the same around at the side. Camouflage netting back there, that's how they concealed it."

"What else have you found?" Braddock asked, grunting as he pushed himself upright.

Lyons came up with him, smiling tightly. "Enough to convince me this was their headquarters," he said. "Two bazookas and about 20 rounds of AP. Explosives, grenades, smoke pots, every type of weapon you can imagine. Target range and armorer's shop set up back there under the cliffs, along the beach. Oh . . . and these." He reached into his pocket and produced an envelope which he handed to Braddock.

The Captain opened the envelope, and quickly glanced through the snapshots.

"The DiGeorge place, Beverly Hills," Lyons explained. "And from every conceivable angle. Bolan obviously plans these things with the thoroughness of a military field commander. It looks as though they did a thorough study of the terrain before they made their hit."

Braddock nodded his head in mute agreement. He started walking slowly toward the house as he placed the snapshots in the envelope and returned the packet to Lyons. "Get those marked and into the lab as soon as you report in," he instructed. "Should be some good latents there. We'll need hard evidence for a conviction . . . all we can get."

"How'd the arraignment go?" Lyons inquired.

They had rounded the corner of the building. Braddock was inspecting a large lean-to of camouflage netting. "Blancanales and Schwartz?" He grunted unhappily. "Got 'em bound over on a couple of misdemeanors. Possession of illegal weapons, illegal use of a radio transmitter. They're already out on bail."

Lyons had raised his eyebrows in surprise. "We had a list of charges a mile—"

"Charges are not convictions, Carl. You should certainly know that much. The fact is, they got old John Grant in their corner and . . . well, you know how it goes."

"Grant comes damn expensive," Lyons observed. He followed the captain onto the patio. Braddock picked up a set of punctured targets and studied them with interest.

"I'd say, the way these are marked, someone has been sighting-in a couple of rifles."

"Where'd they get the money to retain a lawyer like John Grant?" Lyons persisted.

Braddock sighed. "Hell, from their fairy godmothers, I guess. Don't ask me a dumb-ass question like that, Carl. We all know that Bolan's been taking the Mafia's money away from them."

28

"I was just wondering out loud," Lyons mildly replied.

"Well, wonder about this one, then," Braddock said. "We got it on the wire from Jersey that a large trust fund had been set up for the Fontenelli children. Fontenelli, in case you've forgotten, was the first member of the Bolan team to die ... during that Beverly Hills hit."

"I hadn't forgotten," Lyons murmured. He was remembering a tall man, standing in the living room of the Lyons home, soberly passing the time of day with a tow-headed youngster. "Sounds like Bolan is keeping faith with the dead ... and with the young."

"Yeah," Braddock growled. "And I'm not missing any bets. I've got inquiries out on the families of the other dead men ... *Bolan's* dead, that is. I doubt that his tender sympathies would extend to the families of his victims. Anyway, if Bolan is spreading the money around, chances are he's doing it cute enough so that the beneficiaries have legal title to it. That means that he is going through certain legal formalities, and those formalities just might point the way right back to Bolan's present whereabouts."

Lyons nodded his understanding, but added, "After last night, I'd say his tracks are going to get fainter and fainter."

Braddock frowned and turned to stare along the winding drive which connected the house to the road. "How do you reconstruct the thing, Carl?" he quietly asked.

"Well ..." Lyons hitched up his pants and stepped alongside the captain, one arm raised to point out various geographical features as he mentioned them. "We found electronic gadgets monitoring every possible entrance to the property. Schwartz's work, I'd guess. Anyway,

29

the place is wired for sound, and I'd say that their security was top-drawer. I still have no idea how DiGeorge's people located Bolan here, but obviously they did. They tripped the alarms, though, and Bolan was ready for them. We found two burned-out parachute-type flares out there near the road. The lab men are still going over the wrecked vehicles. Preliminary findings indicate that he cut down on them with a high-powered rifle, undoubtedly that Mauser over there." Lyons led his captain to the end of the patio wall and showed him the machine gun. "But now, here's the kicker. Look at the way he has that baby wired up. He provided his own covering fire, see. Juiced this baby up, left it running, jumped into his car, and charged right through their middle to make his getaway. We found deep skid ruts where he tore up the ground getting around the burning vehicles."

Braddock swore softly and knelt to examine the firing lock on the machine gun. "Every day, in every way, I find this guy getting more and more dangerous," he said. He lifted his eyes to the face of his young sergeant. "Suppose we'd tracked Bolan down first, Carl. How many men would it have cost us to take this place?"

Lyons showed a startled frown. "I don't believe Bolan would resist arrest," he declared solemnly.

"You don't, eh?" Braddock grunted to an erect positon and rocked back on his heels, hands gripping the backs of his thighs. "You worry me, Carl," he added thoughtfully. "Some day you're going to put your trust in the wrong . . ."

"It's not a matter of trust," Lyons curtly interrupted. "I've stood face to face with the man, I've talked to him. He's not the usual run of the mill . . ."

"Usual or not, Mack Bolan is a desperate man,"

Braddock cut in heavily. "You get him into a corner and he's going to come out shooting, just like he did here last night. Do you think he asked those people for a password before he started chopping them up?"

"I don't think . . ."

"Then don't talk either!" Braddock said angrily. "I'm trying very hard—*very* hard, Carl, to forget the fact that Bolan escaped us at Balboa in *your* vehicle."

Lyons flushed an angry red, spun on his heels, and went into the house. Scowling, Captain Braddock watched him disappear through the doorway, then he sighed heavily and said, *sotto voce,* "But I *can't* forget, it, Carl. I just can't."

Another thing the captain could not forget was the goal he had been so meticulously pursuing for so many years. Most observers at the Hall of Justice were generally agreed that Big Tim would reach the goal. No other officer on the force seemed to be such a certain candidate for the Chief's chair. Some day, with the kindness of fate and the inexorable workings of the civil service procedures, Big Tim would be the Big Chief. Lately, however, an AWOL soldier who seemed to think he could bring Vietnam tactics to American streets was raising a large question mark around the kindness of Tim Braddock's personal fates. Braddock *had* to get Mark Bolan. A failure now, with the entire nation keeping score, would deal unkindly with a good cop's lifetime design. Braddock *would* get Mark Bolan.

Braddock returned to his car, opened the door, and slid heavily into the seat. He picked up the microphone for the two-way radio, punched the button for the special *Hardcase* network, and established contact with his operations center.

31

"Braddock," he clipped. "Nothing but dead ashes here. I'm coming in."

"Lt. Foster has been wanting to talk to you," he was informed.

"Well, I'm still here," Braddock said wearily.

Andy Foster's monotone bounced back at him. "Definite make, Tim. Shoot-out up near Palm Village late last night. Our boy's handiwork, very plainly."

"Last *night!*" Braddock said savagely. "Why the delay in reporting?"

"The locals had the wrong slant. Tell you about it when you get in. Any instructions?"

"Yeah!" Braddock snarled. "Get a chopper out here to pick me up! You get on over there in a car—no! First, get hold of those people and tell them to keep their fumbling hands off! I don't want them doing *any*thing until I get there!"

"Ten-four."

Braddock sat and fumed, his guts churning. Then he lunged out of the car and roared, "Carl! *Sergeant* Lyons!"

Lyons came running. "Yessir?" he asked breathlessly.

"Get someone to take my car in. Yours too. You'n me are taking a chopper ride."

"Sir?"

"I'm going to give you one more chance to corner the rat. The *rat*, Lyons. Not the new Robin Hood of the West. You understand me?"

"Yessir," Lyons replied meekly. He dropped his eyes and disappeared once again beyond the corner of the building.

Braddock fidgeted and nervously squeezed his hands together. Big Tim's grand design was not quite dead yet. Not, in fact, by a hell of a shot. Mack Bolan was going to be had.

Julian DiGeorge felt his self-control deserting him. He raised veiled eyes to his chief enforcer, Lou Pena, and muttered, "Listen, dammit, I don't want your damn crying excuses! Do you know how close Palm Village is to where I'm sitting right now? Don't give me any vomiting excuses, Lou."

"I don't know what else to say, Deej," Pena replied humbly. "I don't know how the bastard manages it. I just don't know. We got ..."

"I know what you *got*," DiGeorge rasped. "You *got* an old defenseless farm hand and a decrepit old truck. And you *lost* three damn good boys. You *lost*, Lou, you didn't *get* anything!"

"I was going to say, we got a pretty good idea which way he's travelling now. I got people all up and down that highway and ..."

"*Sure* we know which direction he's travelling. He's heading *this* way, Lou. Probably here already. Of course he is! He's here already."

"Hell, Deej, we got thirty boys out there on the grounds. He ain't gonna get through anything like that."

DiGeorge snorted nervously, lit a cigar, and blew the smoke toward the open window. "Just like he *couldn't* get out of that beach house, eh?" He slapped the chair with a flat palm, then did it again.

Pena's eyes followed the trail of smoke out the window. He uncomfortably shifted his weight, coughed, then got to his feet and stood uncertainly awaiting his boss' command. Presently he said, "What d'you think I oughta do, Deej?"

"You're outdated, Lou," DiGeorge said, his voice suddenly mild.

"Huh?"

"I think it's about time you retired."

"Aw hell, Deej, I don't want ..."

33

"*After* you bring me Bolan's head."

"I'll get it, Deej."

"You damn well better. You take five cars, Lou. Full of wild men. And you go over to Palm Village. You shake that place like it never thought of being shook. And you pick up Bolan's tracks. You hear me?"

"I hear you, Deej."

"And don't you come back here without Bolan. You hear me?"

"I hear you, Deej."

"I want Mack Bolan more than I want anything in this world. You understand me, Lou?"

"I understand you, Deej."

"Then get the hell out of here! What are you waiting for?"

Pena got out of there. The boss, he decided, was cracking up. First Bolan was about to walk in the front door, then he was clear over in Palm Village. What the hell did Deej expect of him? It was a senseless question, and Pena recognized it as such even as he thought it. What else? He expected Bolan's head, on a platter, that's what. And Pena, the new chief enforcer, had damn well better get it for him. If he didn't, maybe Pena's own head would end up on that platter. It was not a comforting thing to contemplate. Well, by God, *Pena's* head wasn't going to get on no platter! Deej said to shake the town apart. He'd shake it *down*, by God, if that's what it took. Lou Pena had to get Mack Bolan. There just wasn't any two ways about it. He had to, by God, *get Mack Bolan!*

Chapter Five

THE PLASTICS MAN

Jim Brantzen was one of a vanishing breed of men. Caring little for material wealth and not at all for personal prestige, his major passions of life revolved about dedicated service to those who needed his talents and to the advancement of his own particular branch of medical science. To Brantzen, though, cosmetic surgery was not just a science. It was also an art, and a highly creative one. The balding, middle-aged surgeon disputed the contention that "beauty is only skin deep." Beauty, he knew, is a totality of the personal image, a totality combining character, spirit, and physical appearance in a package that is pleasing to the beholder. He knew, also, the ravages of character and spirit which could be induced by an unpleasing exterior. His own mother had suffered a hideous disfigurement from an accident when Brantzen was a young boy, and in an age when cosmetic surgery was a bumbling science reserved for the very rich. He had seen a once beautiful and vivacious woman curl up and die inside and later die all over as an embittered and totally withdrawn member of society. Jim Brantzen knew the importance of physical beauty, and he knew how much deeper than skin that importance extended. After all these years, he still awoke sometimes from a cold-sweat dream with the muffled sobbing of his mother-in-seclusion tearing at his heart.

Jim Brantzen had heart, and plenty of it. Enough to volunteer for combat-zone surgical duties in Vietnam. Enough to set up his own makeshift hospital in unpacified territory to administer to the torn and disfigured bodies of Vietnamese children, as well as anyone else who happened along. There was a special place in Brantzen's heart for Mack Bolan, also. On various occasions, the tall and seemingly cold Special Missions sergeant had lugged damaged and bleeding children into Brantzen's small field hospital, often through miles of hostile country, and frequently remaining nearby to defend the small outpost against enemy trackers. Brantzen had recognized in Bolan the same sense of dedication to duty which kept the surgeon at his post. Though Brantzen was unalterably opposed to warfare and violence, he could still respect and admire a dedication in that direction. He had even admired the enemy and their tenacious do-or-die approach to their cause, though disapproving of their tactics and disrespect for human life.

Brantzen knew of Bolan's specialty, of course. He knew that the man had been programmed for murder, that he was a military assassin, and he knew how Bolan had earned that tag, "The Executioner." He could still admire him. Indeed, he had to admire him. He had seen him stand up to almost certain death on too many occasions; at the other end of the stick, he had seen the pain-of-soul in Bolan's eyes as he carried broken children into the field hospital. There was no swagger to the man, no story-book bravado; he was a soldier, doing a soldier's job, and doing it with precision and with courage and with dedication. Yes, Jim Brantzen had a deep and abiding admiration for Sgt. Mack Bolan.

He had known also, of course, of Bolan's home-front adventures since his return from Vietnam. He had followed the stories in the newspapers and had wagged his head sorrowfully over the television reports. Some men, Brantzen had decided, just had too much sense of dedication for their own good. If Vietnam had been an unwinnable war, then Bolan's one-man campaign against the Mafia could only be an impossible one. Hounded from both sides, by both the law and the underworld, there could be but one outcome for Mack Bolan. With one tug of his mind, Brantzen had half expected that Bolan would come to him. Another tug told him that it would not happen, that Bolan would stand up one time too many and die on his feet, without once thinking of the refuge which Brantzen could offer him. The surgeon had made a bet between the two sides of his mind, with the odds even as to whether Bolan would cut and run for a new face or stand and die in his old one.

Brantzen had been neither surprised nor disappointed, then, when the Executioner came calling on him. Their greetings were exchanged with an almost formal and subdued warmth, the handshake firm and prolonged, and with few words passing between.

"I've been halfway expecting you," the surgeon said.

"You know why I'm here," Bolan murmured.

"Right. You want me to make you beautiful."

"You could fall dead in the process."

Brantzen grinned. "It shouldn't be all that tough a job."

"You know what I mean, Jim," Bolan said. "My playmates don't like anyone else cutting into the game."

Brantzen had led him through the deserted lobby and into casual living quarters to the rear, small but adequate for the bachelor doctor. "You worry about the playmates," Brantzen told Bolan. "That face of yours is all the worry I can handle at once. Whom do you want to please with the

37

new one, Mack—the old ladies or the young ones?"

Bolan sighed. "You can cut it that close?"

The surgeon smiled at the pun, picked up a sheaf of sketches from a table, and tossed them into Bolan's lap. "I've been working on these ever since I heard you were in the area," he said. "I can give you any of those. It's your choice."

Bolan was shuffling through the sketches. He stopped at one, smiled, passed on, then checked himself and returned to the one that had produced the smile. He laughed softly and tapped the sketch with an index finger. "Did you do this one from memory, or is it just an accident that turned out this way?"

Brantzen bent to study the sketch. He stroked his chin and said, "By gosh, it does look like ... like ..."

"My old sidekick," Bolan said. "And a spitting image. You could really make me look like this?"

The surgeon solemnly nodded his head. "It's not the prettiest of the lot, Mack, but I'll have to agree with your logic. I'd say it's far and away your best choice."

"How soon?" Bolan said, scowling at the sketch.

"If I call right now, my surgical nurse can be here by five," Brantzen replied. "We can be into surgery by six."

Bolan nodded. "The sooner the better," he murmured. "How long, then, before I'm up and around?"

"We can do it with local anaesthesia," Brantzen said. "You'll never have to go to bed, if you'd rather not. And if you're tough enough. I'd like to keep you around for a few days of postcare, though."

Bolan was thinking about it. He said, "I've

been among the wounded before, Jim. It'll have to be that way this time. It's no go if I have to lay around here for days afterward. I have to keep moving."

"I suppose you could," Brantzen replied thoughtfully. "If you're tough enough," he added again.

"How long before the scars are healed?"

Brantzen smiled. "The technique I have in mind will leave only tiny slits here and there, Mack. Except, possibly, for the nose, and I'd say that would be the last to heal. It varies with individuals, of course, but I should say you'd be relatively presentable within a few days to a week. There'll be some sensitivity for quite a while beyond that, though. I'll be doing some plastics work, you know. There could even be some minor rejection problems."

Bolan glanced at his watch. "You say we can get started by six? No chance of an earlier start?"

"Are the hounds at your heels, Mack?" the surgeon asked softly.

Bolan grimaced. "Pretty close," he said. "And I can't hang around here for more than a few hours. I'll have to recuperate on my feet."

"There's going to be pain."

"I've lived with pain before."

"Yes, I'm sure you have. Well ... I could hurry Marge along, I guess, but I'd rather not arouse her suspicions. Come to think of it, this face of yours has been pretty much in the public eye. I guess I'd better have you prepped and ready by the time she checks in. She could never recognize you then."

"We can't just go without her?" Bolan asked quietly.

"Well ..." The surgeon wavered. "It's a ..."

"I've seen you go it alone with the Cong howling all around us."

"Those were emergency conditions," Brantzen said fretfully.

"This isn't?" Bolan asked, grinning.

The surgeon stared at Bolan for a thoughtful moment. He smiled suddenly and said, "Okay, Sergeant, let's get the patient prepped for surgery. Come on, man, move, move, move."

Bolan got to his feet and thrust the sketch at Brantzen. "The patient is ready and waiting, Doctor," he said.

Chapter Six

THE BALANCE

Once a jumping-off spot for hopeful prospectors heading into the Death Valley area, Palm Village had until recently evolved uneventfully into a typical desert-edge trade center serving a sparse agricultural area. Removed from major highway routes and largely untouched by 20th-century progress during the first half of the century, the quiet village had found new life in the desert-land boom of the fifties and sixties. An invasion by promoters and developers had threatened to convert the tranquil community into a second Palm Springs until conservative city fathers invoked legislative powers to cool the pace of progress. As a result, Palm Village was moving calmly along the path of controlled development, retaining much of its original charm while swelling gently into a quiet residential community of retired folk and health-seekers.

The original village square, referred to as "Lodetown," had stoutly resisted all civilizing inroads of the 20th century. It was composed mainly of oldtime saloons and beerhalls which were frequented by farmhands and cowboys from the surrounding area, and was the chief source of Palm Village's crime statistics, most of the trouble developing on Saturday nights and limited to "drunk and disorderlies" and an occasional fistfight. Lodetown boasted a quite stable population of prostitutes, each of them well known by local authorities. All were arrested each Sunday morning, fined $21.20, and released. This was an effective arrangement, considered entirely fair by the girls involved, satisfactory to the demands of law and order, and consistent with the city fathers' concept of "logic and reason." Besides, the weekly fines easily covered the entire expense of policing Lodetown.

Robert (Genghis) Conn was still lean and hard at the age of 52. A tall man with a deeply lined, weathered face, he looked like a Gary Cooper version of the Western marshal. Actually, Conn was chief of the city's small police force and had been a law-enforcement officer since the end of World War II. He had attended the police academy at Los Angeles and had served briefly with the L.A. police, then as an Orange County deputy until recalled to military duty for the Korean conflict. He returned from Korea directly into the chief's job at Palm Village, replacing the one-man agency of Town Marshal in one of the initial acts of civic progress.

It had not been a progressive move for Conn himself, however, and none was more aware of this than Conn. The Palm Village job represented a retreat of the once-ambitious lawman, the desert town offering him the peace and tranquility which had suddenly become so important to him. Conn had seen enough blood and violence to last him a lifetime; he wanted no more of it. For almost twenty years now, he had managed to avoid the violent life. He and his wife Dolly had a modest home with no mortgages in the older section of town, and here they planned to live forever. In peace and tranquility.

On that hot desert morning of October 5th, however, "Genghis" Conn realized that his sabbatical had ended. The pace of progress had caught up to Palm Village; violent death had found its way to his peaceful city. Three dead hoods lay in the coroner's vault at the local funeral home, a hapless old farmhand was barely hanging onto life at Memorial Hospital, and now this big-deal L.A. cop was telling him that his quiet little town was harboring, for God's sake, the Executioner.

"Is it always this hot here?" Captain Tim Braddock complained. He passed a hand across his forehead and squinted into the cloudless sky. "How the hell do you stand it?"

"It's only a hundred and two," Conn replied, lying a little. "This is the cool o' the morning. Wait 'til this afternoon." He pushed open the door to the small building which served as a combination city hall, jail, and police station, and waved his two visitors inside.

Braddock nudged Carl Lyons in ahead; the three lawmen stepped into air-conditioned comfort and moved along a narrow hallway past a door marked CITY CLERK and through a swinging door at the rear. The air conditioning ended here, in Conn's office. Desert coolers filled the window openings. A door of opaque glass and imbedded wire mesh, just beyond an I-formation of desks, opened onto the cell block.

"This the jail?" Lyons asked.

"That's it," Conn replied, jerking a thumb toward the dreary hole beyond the door. "Rarely has any guests ... 'cept on Saturday nights, and then, God, you can't stand the smell of the place. I pour a gallon of pine oil on that floor every Monday morning and just let it set all day."

His visitors had seated themselves; Lyons on a tattered leather couch at the wall, Braddock perching on the edge of a desk. Conn eased into a chair at the center desk, pushed his hat back off his forehead, and said, "What makes you think I got the Executioner in my town, Captain?"

Braddock replied, "Call it a hunch. How many officers on your force, Chief?"

"Twelve," Conn said, his voice a bored monotone. "Besides myself. Run three rotating watch sections, with a light nightwatch." He smiled tiredly. "*Everybody* works on Saturday night, all night long. We only have two cars, only one of *them* is fit to be on the highway. Every once in a while, we double up the watches and give ourselves a decent stretch at home." He grunted and reached for a cigar. "You interested in knowing how much I pay my patrolmen?" Receiving no response other than an embarrassed drop of eyes, he went on: "Myself, I put in a 20-hour day, every day, 'cept once in a while I run Dolly and me into L.A. for a night to ourselves. We get gigglin' drunk, see all the floorshows, and have ourselves a ball with the swingers." The Chief stared at his cigar during a thoughtful pause, then added, "So you think Mack Bolan's responsible for the carrion over at the coroner's."

Braddock shifted his weight uncomfortably and said, "We put out a full poop sheet on Bolan more than a week ago. We were hoping to get the full cooperation from the outlying communities. If you'd just sounded a Hardcase alert last night when the shooting occurred, Genghis, we'd be some valuable hours closer to Bolan right now."

Conn ignored the lightly scolding tone of Braddock's message. "Last night happened to be one of my nights in L.A.," he explained. "As for this Hardcase alert, my night watch just didn't see the thing that way." He bit the end off the cigar, then laid it down and chewed on the plug in his mouth. "Besides we don't have clear jurisdiction. Happened outside of town, you know. 'Bout two miles outside."

Braddock tossed a hopeless glance at his young

sergeant, sighed, and said, "Let me bring a squad in here, Genghis."

Following a short silence, Conn replied, "Okay. On provisions."

"What provisions?"

"You don't bust my town. Meaning, you don't disturb the balance we got here. Law enforcement in this town is strictly *my* business. You want Bolan ... okay, you come in and get him, if you can. But you don't bust my town in the process, and you don't bother any of our citizens."

"Of course," the Captain grunted. "That goes without saying."

"And you march every one of your men in here and let my people get a good look at 'em."

Braddock nodded assent.

"No marked cars, and no uniforms, and you work it quiet ... *damn* quiet."

Braddock sighed and glanced at Lyons. "I just hope we can," he said.

Conn spat the plug of cigar into his hand and raised inquiring eyes to the Los Angeles cop. "Meaning?"

"Meaning that wherever we find Bolan, we're likely to find a convey of Mafia triggermen right close by."

"I want no shooting in my streets, Braddock," Conn said coldly.

"Neither do we," Braddock replied. He arose with a sigh and moved toward the telephone. "Can I use this phone?"

"Reverse 'em."

"Huh?"

"The charges. L.A. is a 45-cent call."

Sgt. Lyons grinned and reached for a cigarette, watching the color flow into his Captain's face. He winked at Chief Conn and lit the cigarette as

45

Braddock's index finger was stabbing into the telephone dial.

"You don't say much, do you?" Conn observed.

The Sergeant exhaled the cigarette smoke, smiled, and said, "No sir." He drew a finger across his throat, rolled his eyes toward the Captain, and sent Conn another wink.

The Chief soberly returned the wink and bit another plug from his cigar. He liked the youngster okay, but that Braddock ... well now, there was something else. Conn did not give a damn about the 45-cent toll call. The youngster realized that, and apparently Big Tim knew it also, judging by the color of his face. But Big Tim also knew that he wasn't going to just walk in and take over Genghis Conn's town. That was the important thing.

Another important thing was occupying Genghis Conn's mind also. If the Executioner *was* in town, there was only one reason why he would be here ... and only one place he was likely to be interested in. This was something the big shot L.A. cop did *not* know. But Genghis Conn knew. And Genghis rather liked the peaceful balance which had been achieved in his town. He had already decided to keep it that way.

Chapter Seven

LOU'S CREW

The Cosa Nostra was the only "family" Lou (Screwy Looey) Pena had ever known. Born in the forbidding slums of East Harlem in the early twenties to a tubercular and dying mother and an imprisoned father, he had been left to more or less shift for himself at a tender age and had grown up as an unofficial ward of the neighborhood. As his mother lingered and his father languished, young Looey ate wherever he could find a place at a table and slept in any crowded bed which would admit him, the tenacious youngster learning early to "live off the streets" and to accept graciously any crumbs tossed his way. It had been a mixed neighborhood of Italians, Jews, and Irish, in which ethnic feuds and rivalries erupted with monotonous frequency. For his first eight years of life, little Looey did not recognize ethnic differences; his hungry belly was receptive to bagels and raviolis alike; a bowl of Irish stew had been his idea of a feast. Pena's life took a dramatic new direction in his eighth year, however, when his dead mama's niece arrived from the old country and took the youngster under her wing. From *Cugina* Maria, then but 22 years of age herself, Pena found an identification of ancestry and learned to be proud of his Neapolitan roots; he also began attending school, at first reluctantly and then feverishly as his young consciousness responded to the challenges of knowledge. During his sixth year of schooling, Maria "moved in with" a member of a neighborhood gang known as "The 108th Street

47

Raiders." She took Looey with her into the new environment; unknown to Maria, Pena immediately quit school (he was then 14) and became a part-time member of the Raiders, working under the tutelage of Johnny "Third Leg" Saccitone, Maria's lover. It was at about this time that the infamous gang wars and underworld intrigues were reaching the climax which would see the firm establishment of the Cosa Nostra families.

Pena served six months in a reformatory at the age of 14, another four months at the age of 15. During this latter stretch, he killed a fellow inmate in a knife fight on the athletic field. He beat this rap by successfully feigning insanity and was transferred to the State Hospital, from where he was discharged at the age of 16. Now wise to the ways of his world, he successfully evaded the reach of the law thereafter and was formally initiated into a Cosa Nostra family somewhere around his 21st year. He was never again arrested or hospitalized throughout a long career as a Mafia "soldier," serving mostly as an "enforcer" and bodyguard to various *Capos*, or family bosses. He had participated in more than a score of murder contracts and had come west with DiGeorge when the latter ascended to the rank of *Caporegime*, or lieutenant, in the early days of the Los Angeles Family. The nickname "Screwy Looey" has stuck with him through the years, but was rarely used to his face. Pena had long been a power in the Western Family, though without official rank until Mack Bolan's execution of DiGeorge's chief enforcer in the Beverly Hills fracas.

Married only to his job and faultlessly loyal to his *Capo*, Pena had received the nod from Di-George to fill the sudden vacancy. Even Pena, however, realized that this promotion had been largely based on a scarcity of qualified candidates. It was generally acknowledged that whatever Pena lacked in brains was more than made up for by his brute strength, stubborn tenacity, and unflagging loyalty to his *Capo*. No one doubted that Screwy Looey would succeed in his new post. More than he himself wanted to succeed, however, he wanted to please Julian DiGeorge. This desire overrode all other considerations. He had vowed to serve up Mack Bolan's head "on a platter" for his *Capo's* extreme pleasure.

Pena arrived in Palm Village on the morning of October 5th in the lead vehicle of a five-car caravan which proceeded directly to the public parking lot at the edge of Lodetown. There they were met by Willie Walker (nee Joseph Gianami), an advance man who had already obtained city permits for "door-to-door selling," and who, moments earlier, had rented an empty store building on the Lodetown square, ostensibly for use as a book crew headquarters.

Willie Walker led the caravan to the alleyway rear entrance to the store and chatted with a uniformed policeman as Pena's soldiers unloaded heavy cartons of "books" from the trunks of the vehicles.

Moments later, with Pena's 25-man crew sprawled about in the comparative coolness of the rented store, Walker reported his conversation with the policeman. "He said it was okay to park in the alley, but we can't block it."

Pena nodded and said, "I'd rather just stay in the cars. At least they're air conditioned. It's hot enough in here to cook us alive."

"The building went with the permits," Walker replied, grinning. "Not much, is it? They got a law here that you gotta be an established firm

49

in this town to do business here. It cost me five a head for the permits, fifty for a week's rent on the store, minimum, and fifty for what they call an associate membership in the Merchant's Association." The grin widened. "And they call *us* racketeers."

"Everybody has to make a living, Willie," Pena growled, dismissing the implied graft. "Well ... hand out those permits and get the kids busy unpacking those boxes. There's hardware and extra ammo under the books."

"Okay."

"Get the books stacked around, make it look good. Put a couple of empty boxes up by the window and let the label show, in case anybody wants to look in and see what we got here." Pena wiped a trickle of perspiration from each temple and added: "Make it quick and get the kids back into those cars. Christ, we'll dehydrate in this dump." He held out a hand. "Gimme some of those business cards, I'm gonna pass some around to our next-door neighbors. Community relations, you know, and it'll give me a chance to look around." He winked, pocketed the cards, and walked toward the front of the building, dragging Walker with him. "Listen, I want one of those big choppers on the floor in each car. And put some books in the back windows, and I want every man with a book in his hand. This has gotta look good. And listen ... I don't want those cars parked in a alley when we're all mobbed up in here. One car in the alley, in case we need it quick ... the others you spot around close. Just make sure they're where we can get to them, and that we're not gonna get blocked off or locked in."

Walker nodded his understanding of the instructions, closed the door behind Pena's departure, and immediately began carrying out the

50

orders. Upon Pena's return some minutes later, the store looked precisely as it was meant to look—like a hurriedly set up center of operations for a crew of itinerant book salesmen. A city map which Walker had purchased for $1.25 from the City Clerk's office was tacked to a wall, on which was being marked the assignment for each squad.

"How long's it gonna take us to cover this hick burg?" Pena inquired.

Willie Walker stared reflectively at the large map. "I'd say we can tap every house in about three to four hours, if we move fast. Five or six if you want it real careful."

"I want it fast," Pena replied. "I just spotted something real interesting over in that parking lot."

"Yeah?" Walker said, his eyes shifting quickly from the map to his boss' face.

"Yeah." Pena was frowning in thoughtful concentration. "Julio's car. Bolan must have dumped it there. I walked past quick and casual. Keys are in it. Blood spots on the seat."

"What's on your mind, Lou?"

"I'm just wondering if the bulls have that car staked out. I saw something else interesting, Willie. Two L.A. cops just walked into the police station."

"Yeah?"

"Yeah. You sure you sold the hicks on our cover?"

"I'm pretty sure."

"You gotta do better than *pretty* sure, Willie."

"Okay, I'm sure. They're sold, Lou. All the guy was worried about was getting his fifty for this shack."

Pena rubbed his nose, glared at the city map, then sighed and said, "Let's get moving. I want Johnny Spiffy to stay with Julio's car, though.

But tell 'im to not fall for no cops' tricks. Make sure he has a picture of this Bolan. Make sure everybody has one. And Willie . . ."

"Yeah, Lou?"

"Make sure everybody understands one thing. We're here to hit this guy Bolan. I don't want no sloppy fingers. Any soldier tells me he *saw* Bolan, and then can't tell me he saw him *dead* . . . well, he just better not come back at all, Willie. You know?"

"I know, Lou. Don't worry. We got the best crew in the country. We'll get this Blacksuit Bolan."

"We better, Willie. Mr. DiGeorge says we better."

"What if the cops get to him first, Lou?"

"Then there'll be some dead cops, too. We ain't backing down to no cops on this hit, Willie. You know?"

The rented store suddenly seemed much cooler to Willie Walker. The veteran Mafia triggerman solemnly nodded his head and replied, "I know, Lou."

Chapter Eight

THE HIT

Mack Bolan was seated comfortably on a leather recliner in Jim Brantzen's living quarters. His hair, which he had bleached on his departure from the East some weeks earlier, was now darkened again to a jet black and the temples lightened with glints of silver. Small plastic discs were affixed to the forehead above each eye and over each cheekbone. A narrow linear shell of the same substance and about one inch long covered each side of his lower jaw, meeting at the chin. An ordinary oversized Band-Aid covered the bridge of his nose.

"How goes it?" asked Brantzen, entering through the doorway from the clinic.

"Great, I guess," Bolan replied, speaking through barely parted lips. "Just don't ask me to get chatty."

"You want some more freeze?" the doctor asked solicitously.

Bolan carefully shook his head and raised a hand-mirror to inspect once again his rearranged features. "Can't believe it's me," he mumbled. "How long before I can get along without these doo-dads?"

"Those 'doo-dads' are a hell of an improvement over being wrapped up like a gift, Mack," the surgeon replied. "Just remember, they're the only thing holding you together."

"Yeah, but for how long?"

Brantzen shrugged his shoulders. "Depends on your recuperative powers. Maybe a week. Maybe two. It's a pressure principle for suturing, Mack.

Beats hell out of stitching. You fool with them, though, and you'll have some damn messy scar tissue. Leave then alone to work their magic and you'll come out of it as pretty and pink as a baby's butt."

"Hard to believe it could be so simple," Bolan commented stiffly, his lips still numbed from the anaesthetic.

"Not so simple," Brantzen said, grinning. "You're going to start feeling like you'd been worked over with brass knucks when that freeze begins to wear off. I removed a bit of bone here and there, mostly from the nose, and added plastic in other areas. It's soft stuff, Mack, sort of like cartilage, and it just *could* start travelling on you. If it does, you beat it back here and let me take care of it. All in all though, the techniques of today are far superior to anything we had just a few years ago. We could, you know, almost put you back just the way you were ... if you ever feel the need of it."

"Or could you change me again?"

The surgeon nodded his head. "Sure. Of course, this sort of tampering with nature shouldn't be overdone." He smiled. "You should see what we can do with a skinny girl's bustline, or hipline, or whatever needs adjusting for that matter."

Bolan tried to smile back but found that his facial muscles would not cooperate. "Next you'll be telling me you've got help for certain male-type problems," he mumbled.

"There's hardly any limit, Mack," Brantzen solemnly replied. "The sort of thing I've done on you is child's play compared to some of the restorative type work I get in here. I didn't have to rebuild tissues on you, you know ... just altered an angle here and there. Still, you have to watch yourself. A bit of carelessness on your part and the whole thing could fall apart. You follow those instructions I gave you, and I mean to the letter."

"There won't be any telltale scars?"

"Not if you follow the instructions. At least, nothing that could be detected by anybody but another plastic surgeon."

Bolan was again staring into the mirror. "It's phenomenal," he said. "Even with the doo-dads, I look just like the sketch. It's just a mask, though, isn't it? A different kind, but still a mask. That isn't me in that mirror."

Brantzen nodded and said, "If you want to get technical, then it's a mask. But a mask you can live behind forever."

"Or fight behind," Bolan said softly.

The surgeon's eyes dropped and he twisted his hands together in some silent emotion. "I sort of thought you'd get that idea," he murmured.

"It's not just an idea, Jim." Bolan dropped the mirror onto his lap. "It's a commitment. I have no choice. I fight until I win or until I die."

"It's 'Nam all over again," Brantzen said sorrowfully.

"That's about what it is," Bolan agreed.

"The meek shall inherit the earth," the surgeon reminded his patient, smiling solemnly.

"Yeah," the Executioner said. "But not until the violent have tamed it." He winced and raised his hands to tenderly probe his cheeks with fingertips.

"You're starting to get the kick?" Brantzen asked him.

"Is that what it is?" Bolan grimaced. "I thought someone just hit me with a baseball bat."

"When it starts feeling like a jackhammer, let me know. I can help you over the rough period."

"Not with junk," Bolan protested.

"Nothing else will help, Mack."

"Then I'll go it alone." Bolan staggered to his feet, grabbing the chair to steady himself. "I've got to keep my mind clear."

"So it doesn't get too meek, eh." Brantzen didn't mean for the comment to sound sarcastic; it did, nevertheless.

"That's right." Bolan checked his machine pistol, ground his teeth against a sudden surge of pain, the slipped in a live clip of ammo. "I've been here too long already," he announced.

"You can't leave here in that shape, man!"

"Hell I can't. I've learned to smell them, Jim. They're around, take book on it."

"They who?" the surgeon asked, though he knew the answer.

"The hounds, the Mafia hounds. They're around, I can feel it."

Brantzen sighed and said, "Yeah, you're right, I guess. They've already been here. I wasn't going to tell you, but ... well ... if you're determined to go out there, Mack, don't stop to talk to any book salesmen."

"That's their trick, eh?" Bolan was getting his gear together.

"That's the trick. The two who were here were very clumsy about it. Offered to donate a set of their books for my waiting room if I'd let them come in and pitch to my in-patients. I told them I was empty at the moment. I am, in fact. Then they ..."

"They tumble to what kind of place this is?" Bolan asked quickly.

Brantzen shook his head. "I doubt that very much. They seemed to think I was running a nursing home or something. Started asking if I'd heard the shooting last night ... if any of my 'old folks' were disturbed ... that sort of stuff. Trying to trip me up, I think, because I'd already told them I was empty. I guess I satisfied them. I saw them going into the house across the way."

"Did you see them *come out?*" Bolan asked, his tone ominous.

Brantzen shook his head in a silent reply.

"Show me the house. Then show me how to get out of here without being seen from that house, and then ..."

Bolan was interrupted by a light rapping at the door. He swung against the wall as Brantzen answered the summons. Bolan caught a quick glimpse of a pretty woman in a white uniform as she announced: "The Chief of Police would like to talk to you, Doctor. Shall I put him in your office, or ..."

Brantzen nodded and said, "I'll be right along," and pushed the door shut. "Goddammit," he whispered. "Genghis Conn has come a'calling."

A flurry of sounds denoting a light scuffle came from beyond the door; then it opened again and a tall man in a khaki uniform stepped into the room, holding a gray desert felt hat in both hands. "I told the little lady it was an unofficial visit, Doc," he said in a soft voice. He smiled genially at Brantzen, then his eyes shifted to Bolan, who was frozen at the wall. The policeman's gaze bounced off the bulge of the weapon, concealed beneath a folded jacket draping Bolan's arm, and returned to the surgeon's flustered countenance.

"Everybody relax," Conn said, still smiling. "I didn't came here to be a hero." The gaze flicked again to Bolan. "Nor to bury one," he added.

"I ... I'm with a patient, Genghis," Brantzen declared testily.

"I can see that." Conn tossed his hat onto a table and dropped his lank frame into a chair. He pulled a cigar from his pocket, took a bite out of it, and continued eyeing Bolan.

Bolan returned to the recliner and eased onto it, half relaxing into the cushions, the jacket still in place across one arm. "It's okay, Jim," Bolan murmured.

The policeman said, "Sure, it's okay. I just stopped by to gab. The doc and I have spent many pleasant moments swapping ideas about war and peace. That right, Doc?"

Brantzen woodenly nodded his head, moved jerkily to a chair, and perched tensely on its edge, his hands clasped across one knee.

"We both abhor violence." Conn laughed softly and took another plug out of the cigar, rolled it into his cheek, and leaned toward Bolan. "Might sound funny, a lawman who wants only peace and tranquility, but ... see ... law enforcement's the only business I know. So ... I came to the desert, looking for the same thing most people seek here. Peace." He laughed again. "I'm not a *law* officer ... I'm a *peace* officer." The eyes twinkled toward Brantzen. "We were talking about that just the other night, Doc ... remember?"

Brantzen again nodded his head. "You run a quiet town, Genghis," he said stiffly.

"Damn right. Mean for it to stay that way, too." The gaze swung to Bolan. "Have you committed any crimes in my town, Mister?"

Bolan said, "None that I can think of."

Conn solemnly moved his head in an agreeable jerk. "That's what I was thinking." He sighed, fiddled with the cigar, and added, "Of course, violence has a way of expanding, squirting into the peaceful zones, running rampant. I wouldn't want that to happen here. You planning on staying in my town long, Mister?"

Bolan said, "I was just leaving."

Conn heaved to his feet. "Give you a lift?"

Bolan exchanged glances with Brantzen. The

surgeon gave a tight nod. "Just follow my instructions to the letter and you'll be all right. A dry icepack will control swelling and reduce pain. Keep it dry, though. And leave the covers until they fall off. If you notice any inflammation around the edges, get to a doctor immediately." He jumped to his feet and pulled Bolan's suitcase from a corner. "I'll help you outside."

"I'm parked out back," Conn advised. He went out the door first, leading the way. Bolan followed close behind, gingerly feeling of his face.

Brantzen overtook his patient, moving alongside as they strolled across the lobby. He thrust a pair of oversize sunglasses at Bolan and said, "You might want to use them. They'll conceal most of the patchwork."

Bolan grunted his thanks and added, in a low voice, "Is this guy for real?"

"I don't know," Brantzen replied in a hoarse whisper. "He's an odd one. Never could figure him. I believe he knows who you are, though."

"Sure he does," Bolan quietly muttered. "Well ... guess I'll just play it by ear. Thanks again, Jim. And take care of that envelope for me, eh?"

The surgeon jerked his head and said, "I was talking to the hospital less than an hour ago. The old man's going to make it."

"Great. He'll need the money." They paused in the doorway. Conn had gone ahead and was opening the car door on the passenger's side. Bolan gripped his friend's hand and said, "Jim ... I don't know how to thank you."

"You thanked me years ago. Just keep an eye on Genghis Conn. There's no telling what he has in mind."

"I'm getting a good feeling about Conn," Bolan said, then he seized the suitcase and walked quickly to the car. Conn took the suitcase off his hands and placed it on the rear seat. Bolan tossed a farewell wave to his benefactor, then slid into the front seat of the police car.

Conn went around and climbed in behind the wheel. "Where to Mister?" he asked quietly.

"That's your decision," Bolan replied tautly. "Your town, Chief, is crawling with undesirables."

"Don't I know it." Conn sighed and started the engine.

The jackhammers were beginning to work over Bolan's face. He stared through the window with a sinking feeling as the big car went into motion and New Horizons slid to the rear. Horizons, Bolan was thinking, never stood still for a moving man. He wondered what lay beyond his next one.

"I'll drop you outside of town, Mister," Conn was saying. "I don't give a damn where you go from there. You can go to hell if you want to, just so it's out of my town, and just so you take your hell along with you."

"No worry there," Bolan quipped. "Hell has a way of following me around."

"I guess you invited it, Mister."

"I guess I did."

The Executioner's hell also had a way of lying in wait for him. The police car had swung around the rear corner of the New Horizons and was straightening into the tree-shaded lane running along the south of the property when a white Chrysler lurched from a secluded driveway and bounced to a halt directly in their path. Another big car pulled across the lane some fifty feet behind them as Conn burned rubber in an arcing halt. Two men leapt from the porch of a house directly opposite Brantzen's clinic and ran a zigzag pattern across the lawn, pistols poised.

"That Goddamn Braddock!" Conn snarled.

Bolan's jacket had already dropped away, revealing the small chattergun. "They're not cops!" he snapped, slumping in the seat and getting a good grip on the door latch. The sudden movement sent shivers of agony into his fast-awakening face.

Conn's gun hand was fighting the flap of his holster when a submachine gun appeared over the hood of the Chrysler and a high-pitched voice sang out, "We want your passenger out on the street where we can get a good look at him. Slowly, slowly. Come out with both hands in sight."

Bolan glanced at Conn and pushed the door open.

"You don't want to go out there, Mister!" Conn hissed.

"Amen," said Bolan.

Conn released his door and cracked it open. "Get ready to hit the deck." Then he was throwing himself sideways toward Bolan and his foot was grinding the accelerator into the floorboard. The big car spurted forward in a wild semi-circle, windshield and window glass shattering under a steady drumfire of heavy-calibre bullets as the chopper cut loose on them.

"You're on your own, Mister!" Conn cried, just as the police car plowed into the Chrysler.

The staccato of the machine gun silenced abruptly. Bolan found himself lying half out of the car. Conn, his door jammed against the Chrysler, was firing his revolver through the shattered windshield. A new volley of fire, this time from the rear, tore through the police car. Conn grunted and said, "Shit, I'm hit."

Bolan drew his legs clear and rolled under the car, passing beneath both vehicles and scooting into the open on the far side of the Chrysler. A large man with a gashed forehead was staggering out of the driver's seat and almost placed a foot on Bolan's chest. Bolan shot him in the mouth as the man gaped down at him, and he had to dodge the falling body. The *Mafioso* with the machine gun was kneeling against the curb, blood trickling from a compound break at the left elbow. He tried to bring the big gun up with one hand. Bolan zippered him from groin to throat with a quick upward sweep of his chattering weapon. He slung his own gun, then, and crawled carefully toward the fallen submachine gun.

Conn was lying in the front seat of the police car, firing sporadically to the rear, from around the doorpost. The two men who had approached from the house were holding cautious cover behind a line of trees some thirty feet to Bolan's left flank; one of them was shouting instructions to the rear vehicle. Bolan scooped up the submachine gun and lay a heavy fire pattern into the distant car, spraying for and finding a hot strike. Flames began licking around the hood, then there was a *whooosh* as fire enveloped the entire vehicle. A blazing figure staggered clear just as the whole thing blew in a roaring explosion.

Conn yelled "Bingo!" and began plunking shots toward the trees. Bolan abandoned the machine gun and moved out in a flanking maneuver with his lighter chattergun. The two men broke their cover, fleeing toward the house. Bolan was vaguely aware that Genghis Conn had moved with him, leaving his wrecked vehicle and moving rapidly across the street to the line of trees.

The resuming chatter of Bolan's light weapon was eclipsed by the sudden *balooom* of a shotgun. One of the fleeing men crumpled in midstride and crashed to the ground in a lifeless heap. The shotgun roared again and the second man was flung about in a flopping tumble. Conn stepped back into the street, smoke still curling from both barrels of the shotgun, and stared silently at Mack Bolan.

Bolan slipped a fresh clip of ammo into his gun and walked slowly toward the lawman. "Good shooting," he said quietly, "... for a *peace* officer."

Conn grinned and his eyes turned to a quick appraisal of the battle zone. "Damn, that was quick," he said in an awed voice. The right side of his khaki shirt was wetly red.

"How bad are you hit?" Bolan asked him.

"Not as bad as it feels, I guess," the lawman replied. "I'll just step back over to Doc Brantzen's and let him take a look." He was moving toward the police cruiser. "Think that Chrysler will run?" he asked Bolan.

"It looks all right," Bolan said.

"Okay. What I said goes. You're on your own. I'll give you a one minute jump. Then I'll have to call in. But listen ... show up in my town again, I'll shoot you on sight." He was easing himself carefully into the cruiser and searching for the radio microphone. "Off the record, Mister, I admire your guts. But I wouldn't give two cents for your future, new face or no."

Bolan said, "Thanks," and dragged his suitcase from the rear seat, tossed it into the Chrysler, pulled carefully away from the cruiser, and made his exit with a squeal of tires. In his rearview mirror, he saw Jim Brantzen running across the grounds of New Horizons, heading for the police car, a medical bag in his hand.

Bolan took the corner with a fishtailing swing, straightened out, and unleashed the power of the big car. The pain and the excitement had got-

63

ten to him. He ran a hand inside his shirt, probed carefully along his ribs, and came out with reddened fingers. In addition to everything else, he had been hit. He felt unreal, giddy, and suddenly very weak. Bolan fought down a wave of nausea and forced himself to concentrate on a way out of town. Little demons with tiny flame-throwers were working themselves into the bone above his eyes and sending pulsating bolts of hell down into his nose, flaring into his cheekbones, and along the jaw ridges. The throbbing slice along his ribs seemed pleasurable by contrast.

He remembered something Flower Child Andromede, one of his Death Squad dead, had said once: "Hell is for the living."

Mack Bolan knew where his new horizon was leading him.

It was the Horizon to Hell.

Chapter Nine

THE IMBALANCE

According to the official record, the October 5th bloodbath at Palm Village was sparked when the Chief of Police was stopped at an illegal roadblock on the eastern edge of that city. Aware that his small desert town had become the object of a search for the infamous Mack Bolan by a special detail of Los Angeles police as well as by "triggermen from an L.A. mob," Chief Robert (Genghis) Conn stated that he had at first thought the roadblock to be the work of the special police detail headed by Los Angeles Captain of Detectives, Tim Braddock, but that "it immediately thereafter became clearly evident that I had happened into a Mafia dragnet for this Bolan character."

Upon questioning by reporters, Chief Conn was unable to explain how he had single-handedly slain the eight gunmen at the scene, who were armed with two submachine guns as well as a variety of other weapons. "At a time like that, who's thinking?" Conn remarked. "It's a matter of reflexes and instinct. I'm as surprised as anyone that I came out of it with only a scratched rib."

Several newsmen, in filing their reports, hinted that the full story had not been revealed, pointing out the similarity of this initial battle at Palm Village with other known episodes involving Mack Bolan, the Executioner. The ensuing action in that previously peaceful city proved more typical of police-gangster confrontations and shootouts. Responding to Chief Conn's alarm, three cars of the special LAPD detail which converged on the scene flushed another group of supposed book salesmen (later identified as Cosa Nostra "soldiers," as was the first group) who had been canvassing a neighborhood several blocks to the west of the first encounter.

"They (the book salesmen) opened fire first," said Sgt. Carl Lyons of the L.A. detail. "I wouldn't even have noticed then otherwise. Apparently they had heard the fireworks from Genghis Conn's shootout and, misreading it as a hit on Bolan, were trying to divert us from the scene. There was just myself and Patrolman Hank Edwards in my car. We were sprayed by an automatic weapon from pointblank range, and Edwards lost control of the car. We rolled, and I guess that's what saved us. There were five gunmen in the attacking force, and they had quite an arsenal. The overturned cruiser gave us good cover and the radio was still operational. We had help in a matter of seconds. Three of the hoods were killed at the scene, one surrendered with a flesh wound in the leg, and another tried to escape in their vehicle. He ran right into Captain Braddock at the first intersection and was killed in the collision. The Captain got out of it with only a wrenched shoulder. I guess the single gunman who managed to break out and flee from the shootout with Conn just kept on going. No . . . we have no idea of his identity."

The Palm Village toll so far: 12 Mafia dead, 1 arrested; 3 policeman lightly wounded; 2 private automobiles destroyed; 1 Palm Village official vehicle moderately damaged; 2 LAPD cars heavily damaged. The worst was yet to come.

While most of the law enforcers in the city were still at the scenes of the earlier battles, a Palm Village foot patrolman, alerted to the hostile forces encamped in that city, had become suspicious of a man in a dark, late-model Lincoln Continental which had occupied the Municipal Parking Lot for most of the morning. The patrolman had noticed that the man had been paying rapt attention to an almost identical vehicle in a closeby space. The second vehicle had been ticketed for overparking, by that same officer. "Every time I showed the least interest in that 'overpark' this guy in the other car got agitated," the patrolman later reported. "Finally I just went over and invited him out of the car. I just wanted to see his driver's license so I could identify him later, in case something turned up, you know, but when I got a good look at the guy's face I started deciding I'd better shake him down good first. I just didn't like his looks. Well, he came out of that car fighting mad. He didn't pull no gun, not at first, but he tried to knee me. I sort of twisted around that, but I caught the knee in my gut and it sort of knocked the wind out for a second. But I rapped him across the elbow with my club, and I was down on one knee there, and the next thing I know I'm looking up the barrel of a gun. I don't know why it didn't tear my face off. He was so close when he fired that I got powder burns, and the Doc is still a little worried about my eyes— but believe it or not, he missed me. I heard the bullet sing past my ear, but I guess I still thought I was hit. I couldn't see much and there was a lot of pain in my face. Well, I went down ... holding my face in my hands. Then I realized right away I wasn't really hurt and I came right back up again. The guy was running across the street. I saw him going around the corner into Lodetown and I ran after him. I saw him disappear into the old Brown's Mercantile, an empty store there. He was with those other people, those book people.

I'd just been talking to them a couple of hours earlier, and they'd seemed like all right guys. Well, I was running on over to headquarters to get some reinforcements when I bumped into Gene Perkins, one of our patrolmen. Gene was off duty and downtown with his wife, doing some shopping. He sent me on to headquarters and he tore off for Brown's Mercantile. Headquarters was deserted when I got there. It took me a minute or two to raise the Chief on the radio. And then I guess I passed out. The Doc says I got a light concussion out of that blast in the face."

The narrative continues, as picked up by Patrolman Gene Perkins: "I saw this big black car easing out of the alley behind Brown's just as I was arriving at the scene. I was on foot and I wasn't in uniform, but I always carry a gun. I have a special off-duty revolver I carry in a swingout holster under my jacket. My wife always used to rag me about wearing that gun around—you know, she called me Joe Friday—but a police officer is always on duty, he's never really off. Well, I stepped out in the street with my gun drawn, and I signal for this car to stop. Instead of stopping, he throws into reverse and scoots back inside the alley. I see two men in the front seat, and I think one or two were in the back. I fire a shot in the air and yell for them to halt. I'm running toward the alley, see, and just about the time I get there, they're coming out again, fast this time, and I hear it even before I see it, so I know what's coming. I jump the curb and whirl up against the side of Al's Bar and Grill—I'm standing maybe ten feet from the alley when they come busting out. I put a shot right through the wing vent window and I have to say, the guy has quick reflexes. He stands that big job on its nose, he's not even completely clear of the alley yet, and he's in reverse and gunning backwards again. Meanwhile I'm flat on my belly and getting as small as possible—these guys are returning my fire!

"Soon as they're out of sight again, I'm scrambling to my feet and I'm peering around the corner of the building. They're already halfway to the other end of the alley, and wouldn't luck have it, there's a beer truck down behind Molly's Joint, blocking the alley. They're sealed in, see. This one gunman jumps out of the back seat and he's yelling at the guy unloading the beer truck. The beer driver is ignoring him and going on about his business. I pump a shot through their grill just to keep the pressure on. Then this guy that was doing all the yelling is back there clubbing the truck driver with his gun. I see it, plain as day, from less than half a block away. The one with the gun is climbing up into the cab of the truck. I'm getting plenty of return fire, don't worry about that. Those guys have a chopper down there, and they're using it, so I'm forced to shoot with my left hand around the corner of the building, so I'm not exposing myself. I never tried lefthanded firing before—call it a lucky shot with that little snubnose .32—but I drilled that hood as he was standing behind the wheel of the beer truck. He falls back into the alley. Then another piece of luck came my way. Or don't call it luck, call it civic spirit and supporting your policemen. Old John Trappolino, lives down on the south side, retired bricklayer, I think, comes into Lodetown every day about that time for a quiet glass of beer and a couple of games of shufflebowl at Al's place. Usually parks right there on Second Street, at the side of Al's. I guess John saw what was going on. Anyway, all of a sudden here he comes in that little Rambler of his, just easing along in low gear, his door open. I see John stepping out of the car and it's still moving, like he was a teen-ager, that nimble you know. The Rambler jumps the curb right behind me and heads into that alley at an angle and it hits the wall of the Village Bakery and dies there, angled into the alley and corking it good.

"Well, these guys in the black car aren't going to be going anywhere for now, for sure. They abandon the car and they're scampering through the back entrance of Brown's Mercantile when I hear the sirens tearing toward Lodetown. I guessed that Arthur, the other patrolman, was sending me some help. I can tell you with no feeling of shame at all that I was damn glad to hear them coming. I'm running for Main Street now, and people are all out in the street trying to see what's happening. This hampers me a little, but I still round the corner just as the front door to Brown's opens and a guy pokes his head out. I throw a shot at him. It misses, but takes out the window behind him and this serves the purpose. He thinks they're covered front and back, see, and he dodges back inside the store, and I'd have given a nickel for their thoughts about that time. Then the Chief and the Hardcase cops arrive, and we've really got them sealed in there now. They died hard, though. I wouldn't want to die that way."

October 5th was the day that Lodetown burned to the ground, every building on the four blocks around the square being leveled in a spectacular fire that was immediately beyond the control of the small fire department. It is known that the blaze originated in the interior of an ancient structure which had originally housed a general store known as Brown's Mercantile Company, and which had been short-term rented only that morning to a Mafia cadre posing as book salesmen. It was suspected that the fire had been deliberately set by the three unidentified underworld figures who had taken refuge in the building, possibly intended to create confusion and thus provide a diversion for their escape. If this was the intent, then the plan backfired on its perpetrators. Their charred bodies, burned beyond any possibility of identification, were found near the rear door of the building.

At the height of the fire, another shootout occurred between police and "two carloads of gunmen" in the street adjoining Lodetown. The running battle erupted when Captain Tim Braddock spotted the two vehicles cruising "in obvious curiosity" past the scene of the conflagration. Braddock identified one of the occupants as Lou "Screwy Looey" Pena, a long-suspected Mafia "enforcer" in the DiGeorge Family. Three of Braddock's officers were found wounded in this encounter, one seriously, and an innocent bystander, a familiar Lodetown figure known only as Indian Joe, was caught in the crossfire and killed. The two vehicles made good their escape, aided by the confusion attending the fire, and were later found abandoned in another section of the city. Dried blood was found in both automobiles, indicating that some of the police bullets had found their marks.

All in all, the full toll of the Battle at Palm Village was a fearful one: 32 commerical buildings, old but still functional and housing thriving businesses were destroyed, 26 private automobiles were burned to a total loss. Surprisingly, there were no human casualties of the fire, other than those previously noted. But Lodetown, a quaint if somewhat bawdy reminiscence of the Old West, suddenly ceased to be. The "balance" of Genghis

Conn's town had been overturned. Upon the site of Lodetown would arise a modern business complex with no room for lonely farmhands and their naughty companions of the night. A new tax structure would necessarily emerge from the transformation; the Palm Village police force would become updated, more responsible, less "peaceful."

Staring solemnly at the ashes of Lodetown some hours later, Genghis Conn confided to Doctor Jim Brantzen: "It had to happen, Doc. Your friend was the catalyst this town needed . . . and that *I* needed. I'm sorry . . . I'm sorry for all the loss of life and property, but . . . at the same time . . . I'm not sorry. If you ever see that friend of yours again, tell 'im that Genghis Conn has no regrets."

"I'll tell him that . . . if I ever see him again," the surgeon replied.

Big Tim Braddock, returning to Los Angeles with his junior officer, Carl Lyons, offered a contrasting view. "You can see what a disaster this Mack Bolan is, Sergeant," he growled. "I hope I never again hear any Pollyannish nonsense out of you concerning the virtues and social values of this feud of his. He brings out the worst in everything he touches. We've got to get that guy! We've got to get him before he sends the whole damn state sliding into the sea!"

"It's a damn shame," Lyons replied faintly.

"What?"

"I said it's a damn shame," the Sergeant repeated, his voice growing stronger. "It's a shame that Bolan has to take the rap for all of *our* mistakes."

"*Whose* mistakes?" Braddock said angrily.

"Ours. All of us. You and me and John and Jane and all of us straight citizens. Bolan's no disaster, Cap'n, no more than a compass is the North Pole. You can fire me if it'll give you any comfort, but if you and I were good enough cops ... then there wouldn't be any Bolan. Bolan's no disaster, Cap'n. He's an indictment. He's indicting you and me and society at large, for malfeasance and gross ..."

"That's enough of that!" Big Tim roared.

"Not even nearly," Lyons quietly replied.

They drove in silence for a moment, then Braddock said, "You're out, Carl. I guess I can't blame you for your own personal feelings. I mean, I guess I can understand. But those feelings disqualify you for Hardcase. I'll turn in your release tonight."

"Thanks," Lyons said. "But it's probably an unnecessary formality. Somehow I feel that we'll never see Bolan again."

"How's that?" the Captain asked.

"I don't know." Lyons sighed heavily. "I just feel that we've witnessed the end of an era. I think Hardcase is dead by default."

Braddock shifted his weight uncomfortably, reached for a cigarette, and growled, "Over my dead body, buddy. I'll see that bastard behind bars or I'll turn in my badge."

"Hope you'll enjoy your retirement," Lyons muttered.

"What?"

Lyons slumped over the wheel of the speeding vehicle and peered doggedly ahead. "I was just thinking out loud," he said. "I still think this is the end of an era."

"We'll see about that," Braddock said.

Sgt. Lyons was partially correct. The Palm Village episode did mark a turning point for the Executioner. But it was a turn into eclipse, not into extinction. Mack Bolan, behind his mask, was

73

about to enter the most meanacing and suspenseful stage of his adventures against the Mafia. He had decided to "get inside" Julian DiGeorge's Western family ... and the Executioner's mask was going to put him there.

Chapter Ten

THE LAMBRETTA MASK

Ten days had elapsed since the fracas at Palm
Village and still Lou Pena had not returned to the
Palm Springs estate of Julian DiGeorge. A brief
message had come back on the evening of October
5th carried by a painfully wounded Willie
Walker: "Lou says to tell you he'll be back when
he's got Bolan's head in a sack."

DiGeorge promptly doubled his palace guard
and spent several days in cautious seclusion. On
October 10th, he summoned the convalescing
Walker to his chambers and questioned him again
concerning the events at Palm Village.

"Maybe the guy *is* dead," DiGeorge commented
at the conclusion of the interview, alluding to
Mack Bolan. "Maybe one of those unidentified
bodies was his. Maybe the cops are playing it
cozy, trying to keep the heat on us."

"I don't know about that," Willie Walker told
DiGeorge. "From what I could make out, Bolan
wasn't even in that town. We found Julio's car,
like I said, but the way I make it Bolan just dumped
the car there and stole another one on his way out.
It don't make sense that he would dump the car
and then hang around waiting for us to find it."

"Don't try to figure Bolan," DiGeorge warned
his triggerman. "He likes to think he's tricky, so
don't try to say what he would do and what he
wouldn't do. You know the town, Willie. Soon as
you're up and around good, I want you to take a
few boys over there and give everything another
quiet look-see. Plan it any way you want, but get

75

some questions answered. If Bolan *is* dead, I damn sure want to know it. You understand?"

"I understand, Deej," Willie Walker assured the *Capo*.

During the following few days, DiGeorge had begun to relax somewhat. He went to Acapulco in his private plane on October 12th, combining a pleasant holiday with an urgent business conference which had been hurriedly requested by a Mexican associate. The discussion centered around the new U.S. border crackdown on narcotics traffic, and ways of circumventing this crippling interference with the multi-million dollar business. Returning by way of San Diego, he conferred there briefly with Anthony "Tony Danger" Cupaletto, *Caporegime* of the California border territory, to pass on the new strategy for the acquisition of Mexican heroin and marijuana.

When Cupaletto tactfully questioned DiGeorge regarding the status of Mack Bolan, the Mafia boss expressed the conviction that the last had been seen of "big bad Bolan." He suggested that Tony Danger "worry more about the Border Patrol and less about fancy ghosts."

"You just get the business communities to screaming about their lost bucks," DiGeorge added. "The Feds think they're pressuring *us* . . . you show them what real pressure is. Morales is working the other side of the border. You link up on this side and get the straight businessmen to howling about this harrassment of border traffic. In the meantime, we'll rely on the boats to get the stuff in."

The Family was going on with business as usual. As he returned to Palm Springs, DiGeorge's mind was busy with the problem of succession to the Number Two, or "underboss" spot which had been vacant since Bolan's execution of Emilio Giordano in September. Tony Danger was not even a candidate in DiGeorge's thinking. Bolan had executed the most promising lieutenants of the hierarchy. DiGeorge realized that a decision would have to be made quickly to avoid the possibility of ambitious intrigues among his underlings. Rank in the Cosa Nostra meant much more than mere position and prestige; it represented raw power and pyramiding fortunes in what some federal officials were already beginning to refer to as "the invisible second government of the nation."

Bolan's traumatic punches at the organization had produced a more far-reaching effect, DiGeorge knew, than probably Bolan himself even realized. Normal attrition through an occasional death or arrest within the ranks had never posed too much of a problem for the strongly organized and formally administered combine. Intra-family disputes and "licenses" came under the exclusive jurisdiction of that family's *Capo*; he was a boss whose slightest whim was enforced by a life-or-death disciplinary code. DiGeorge could not remember a time since the Maranzano-Genovese wars of the thirties when there had been such a high attrition rate within a Cosa Nostra family. Thanks to Bolan, the hierarchy of DiGeorge's family was now a shambles.

Things were bad even at the crew level. DiGeorge smiled wryly, thinking of Screwy Looey Pena as his Chief Enforcer. Screwy Looey had been a good soldier. DiGeorge had no doubt that he would forever be a good *soldier*, loyal to the death, but he simply did not have the stuff for rank. Where would DiGeorge go to fill his vacancies? The families had been closed to new members for years and there was a notable absence of young new blood in the organization. Oh, there were young *employees*, sure, but hell, you couldn't give an *employee* rank. DiGeorge filed a mental

77

note to raise the issue with the *Commissione,* the national Cosa Nostra ruling council, at the first opportunity. Meanwhile, he would have to wrestle alone with the problems of succession.

DiGeorge's reception at Palm Springs on October 15th reflected the tenor of the times. Six vehicles, including an armor-plated Cadillac, awaited him at the private hangar. The reception committee numbered 26, but was headed by a long-haired "soldier" known as Little John Zarecky. Obviously nervous and awed by the great man's presence, Zarecky stammeringly reported to DiGeorge that Pena had not been heard from and that Willie Walker had departed "with a crew" two days previously. This left the palace guard without a ranking commander; Little John had been left in charge. DiGeorge immediately passed the mantle of authority to Philip "Honey" Marasco, a 41-year-old bodyguard who had accompanied him on the Mexican trip. Thus it was that DiGeorge had no one to bring him up to date on the happenings at home as the motorcade wended its way to the sprawling Palm Springs villa, and thus it was that Julian DiGeorge had no inkling of the existence of the man called Frank Lambretta until the startling confrontation on DiGeorge's poolside patio.

The pool and patio occupied a "private" area of the villa, a preserve stormily demanded some time earlier by DiGeorge's widowed daughter, Andrea DiGeorge D'Agosta, who strongly resented the presence of "hoods and goons" in the family home. Andrea, who had been ignorant of her father's underworld connections until the Bolan adventures, was also nurturing an ill-concealed resentment of DiGeorge himself, and the two had been all but estranged during the weeks since DiGeorge's exposure as a Cosa Nostra boss.

DiGeorge was not particularly surprised to find Andrea at the pool. Indeed, she had been spending most of her daylight hours there since the incident at Beverly Hills—"mooning around," as DiGeorge put it, "and wishing we could get the spilt wine back in the broken bottle." What did surprise and shock him was the inescapable fact that his daughter was technically naked and that, moreover, she was entertaining a strange man who was in about the same state of undress.

"You *slut* you!" was DiGeorge's homecoming salutation to his daughter.

The man in the case was clad only in a pair of wet jockey shorts. He was lying face up on a sunning board. Andrea, wearing only the scanty bottom half of a bikini, was lying atop the man in a tight embrace. She raised her face to her father and said, "Poppa! Turn your head!"

"I'll turn *your* head right offa your shoulders!" DiGeorge howled. "Get up offa there and get your clothes on!"

In a voice choked with embarrassment and anger, the girl insisted, "I'm not moving until you turn your head!"

"Yeah, that's right," the unhappy father roared. "You'll show your bottom to any two-bit bum that happens past, but your Poppa's gotta turn his *head!*" He had already turned away, however, rocking angrily on the balls of his feet and squeezing his hands together in frustrated rage. "Who's the bum?" he yelled.

Andrea's voice was shaking as she replied, "I'm not talking to you, Poppa, until you calm down. And Frank is not a bum. We're going to be married, in fact, and ... and ..." She lost her voice completely and was having trouble hooking herself into the bikini top. A small girl, just over five feet tall and weighing hardly a hundred pounds,

79

she made up in quality of what she lost in quantity, with all the planes and angles which have made Italian beauties the sex symbols of the world.

Her "partner in crime," as she laughingly referred to him later, exhibited no reaction to her "we're going to be married" line. He rolled easily off the sunning board and pulled on a pair of white Levi slacks, smiled faintly at the girl, then went over to the brooding figure of her father.

"I'm Frank Lambretta, Mr. DiGeorge," he quietly announced.

DiGeorge inspected him through veiled eyes. He saw a tall man, lithe, muscular, maybe 30 or 35, a bit too damn good-looking. A playboy, maybe. The Springs were full of them. DiGeorge felt cheapened by his daugher's indiscretion. He let go a disgusted snort and delivered a stinging backhand slap to the man's face. The tall man obviously saw the blow coming but he stood and received without flinching. A four-finger imprint showed a pale contrast to the smooth flesh surrounding it; a muscle bunched in the jaw and a nerve rippled the flesh beneath the eye.

"I guess you figure I had that coming," the man said. He spoke slowly, obviously laboring for self-control. "But that was your first and last free swing. Be advised."

"Yeah, yeah," DiGeorge muttered, "I'm scared to death with your advice."

The girl had succeeded in covering her heaving bosom and was marching toward her father with fire in her eyes. "You're a nut, a *nut!*" she cried. "You go all holy over an innocent thing like this while all the time you're standing there a murderer, and a thief, and a . . ."

Grunting with rage, DiGeorge had been pushed too far and had let loose another slap, this one aimed at his daughter. She, too, saw it coming and ducked back, cutting off her accusations with an alarmed yelp, but the man called Lambretta had reacted even faster. His hand shot out and imprisoned the infuriated DiGeorge's wrist, abruptly arresting the swing and holding the stiffened hand like a vibrating leaf directly in front of DiGeorge's eyes.

The two men glared into each other's eyes for a tense moment, the silence of the struggle unbroken until Lambretta whispered, "Give the kid a break, Deej."

"I'll give her a broken head," DiGeorge hissed.

"Call it all my fault," Lambretta suggested in a barely audible voice, still gripping the other's wrist. "I pressured her into it. Now let it go at that."

"You let go my wrist!"

"If I do, and if you go for the kid, Deej, I'll drop you in the pool. Now stop being old-country." Lambretta released his grip and moved a pace backwards, smiling faintly at the outraged father.

"Do you know just who you're talking to, punk?" DiGeorge snarled.

Lambretta jerked his head in a curt nod. "Yes, I know who I'm talking to. And it still goes. If I have to dunk you to cool you off, then get ready for a swim, Deej."

Suddenly aware that he had been repeatedly called "Deej" by the brash interloper, DiGeorge stared at his tormentor more closely and asked, "Where do you get off calling me Deej? What'd you say your name is?"

Andrea began giggling in the sudden letdown of dangerous tensions. DiGeorge threw her an angry glare, then stomped his foot and opened his arms to her. "Aw, come on, come on," he said forgivingly.

The girl stepped into his arms and began crying on his shoulder. The tall man returned to the sunning board, sat down, and snared a pack of Pall Malls from the flagstones. He lit a cigarette and got into socks and shoes. DiGeorge and the girl approached the sunning board, arms linked, smiling at each other self-consciously.

"Maybe it takes something like this to break up an iceberg," DiGeorge was saying to his daughter. "It's been weeks since you'n me were pals." He nudged Lambretta with his toe and said, "So whoever said it was any fun being a young widow, eh? When's the wedding? How long you two been making it big like this, eh?"

Andrea said hurriedly, "We haven't set the date, Poppa."

"You better set it," DiGeorge said humorously, ". . . from the looks of things when I walked up."

Lambretta smiled around his cigarette and rose to his feet. He put on his shirt, then extended an open hand to the older man. "Friends?" he said simply.

"Hey, a handshake for the future father-in-law?" DiGeorge protested. He bypassed the hand, grasped Lambretta's arms, and planted a noisy kiss on his cheek.

Andrea giggled, said, "I'd better get dressed," and raced toward the door.

DiGeorge watched her out of sight, then his smile faded and he stepped quickly away from the other man, inspecting him with a suddenly critical eye. "You better be able to stand a close investigation, Mister hopeful son-in-law," he said ominously.

Mack Bolan smiled through his Lambretta mask and said, "You can get as close as you like, Dad."

82

Chapter Eleven

THE COVER

In the curious old-world formality still found in Mafia circles, pride and respect could be considered as the basics of any human relationships in that society. Indeed, it was rare for even a *Capo* to openly insult the lowliest of his cadre; it was a serious offense, subject to trial before a kangaroo court, for any member to "lay hands" upon another in anger, and one of the charter rules was that a man's wife was inviolable by others of the organization. Mack Bolan was aware of this curious code of conduct—curious mainly because of its framework of crime and violence. He would not have deliberately chosen such a far-out introduction to *Capo* Julian Di-George, couched as it was in such strong overtones of disrespect and humiliation: one does not win *Capos* and influence *Mafiosi* by trampling all over their sensitivities, was Bolan's own assessment of his bold *faux pas*, but the thing had been done, could not be undone, and perhaps it would turn out to be the best of all possible introductions.

Andrea had changed quickly into colorfully appealing hiphuggers and tight nylon blouse, returning to the patio just as her father was leaving by another exit. She gazed shyly at the man she knew as Frank Lambretta and said, "Poor Poppa, I could have spared him that."

"I guess he'll live through it," Bolan said, smiling. "If *I* can, *he* can."

The girl laughed melodiously and carefully seated herself in a deck chair, her eyes remaining steady on Bolan. "I guess I *do* owe you an apology," she said. "*And* a note of thanks. I'm sorry I had to spring that marriage routine. I was just thinking of Poppa's feelings. If you . . ."

"It's okay," Bolan interrupted. "We can carry the gag along for a while if you'd like."

The girl soberly nodded her agreement. "I was about to say, if you wouldn't mind playing the charade for a while it would save me an awfully messy situation. Poppa is a bit old-worldly about such things."

Bolan showed her the winning Lambretta smile and said, "Can I pick you up for dinner?"

She was staring at him fixedly as she shook her head in a slow negative. "You're forgetting your family obligations," she told him in mock sobriety. "Poppa will be expecting you for dinner, here, so make it by eight, please, jacket and tie."

"Eight it is," he replied, grinning.

She abandoned the chair and went into his arms, lifting her lips in a breathless invitation. He accepted the offering. She sighed into his mouth then wriggled loose and nuzzled his throat. "The weather's pretty warm down here," she whispered. "Don't worry about dinner. Maybe we can go somewhere *after*."

Bolan patted her bottom, released her, and walked toward the exit DiGeorge had cleared moments earlier. He turned to wave a farewell but the girl was already disappearing around a corner. Bolan went on out, passing through a narrow archway and into the parking area at the side of the villa. A chunky man in a Palm Beach suit, whom Bolan had not seen during any of his frequent visits to the villa over the past several days, rounded a corner of the building, moving fast toward a parked car. The man did a double-take at Bolan and said, "Who the hell are you?"

"I'm sure you'll find that out without my help,"

Bolan replied pleasantly. He slid behind the wheel of a gleaming Mercedes, cranked the powerful engine, and spun out with a spray of gravel.

The man in the Palm Beach was still staring after him as he stopped for clearance through the gate, a mere formality in view of Bolan-Lambretta's now-familiar presence at the DiGeorge country estate.

Not until the villa was a half mile behind did Bolan readjust the mirror for an inspection of his face. He probed the tender tissues with careful fingers, wincing at contact with the area that had fallen under DiGeorge's stinging slap. It had required all his self-control to maintain a steady visage during that moment of incredible pain. He was hoping now that no interior damage had been done. Things were working out too well to have his face crumble on him. Yes ... things were working out. He thought of Andrea, and knew a mixture of pleasure and regret. It had, of course, been a completely casual relationship ... with no questions asked and none wanted. He had no reason to feel guilty about his opportunistic cultivation of the girl. She had been ready for a tumble ... it could have been Bolan or anybody, so why *not* Bolan? He was using her, sure, but then she was using him also. This much was patently clear. She had *wanted* DiGeorge to find them in that compromising scene. She was using Bolan to strike back at her father, to hurt him. Okay. So Bolan was doing the same thing with her, and with the same target in view.

These thoughts carried him back to his hotel. He went directly to his room, showered, changed to a light suit, and buckled on his side harness with the snap-out revolver. Then he went down to the desk, nodded at the clerk, an ever-smiling and always immaculate man of about forty, and placed a twenty-dollar bill on the counter. "Who's been asking about me?" Bolan asked the clerk.

The clerk eyed the money, then raised a veiled gaze to his guest. "Has someone been asking about you, Mr. Lambretta?" he asked drily.

"That's what the twenty wants to know."

"As a matter of fact ..." The man drummed his fingers on the counter and smiled cautiously. "... A man was in here less than an hour ago who seemed to have an interest in you, Mr. Lambretta."

"What did you tell him?"

The clerk's eyes fell again to the twenty-dollar bill. He smiled and said, "Well, really ... what is there to tell, Mr. Lambretta? You're registered here. You deal in cash, not credit cards. You're quiet, mind your own business, and ..." He flashed Bolan a hopeless look.

"And I lay a hundred on the ponies every morning with my friendly local bookmaker," Bolan added.

The clerk's eyes darted to left and right but the smile did not leave his face. "Loose talk is not very sporting, Mr. Lambretta," he said nervously. "I'd appreciate it if you wouldn't speak so casually of such, uh, connections."

Bolan retrieved the twenty, leaned away from the desk and unbuttoned his coat, allowing it to stand open to reveal the snubbed .32 nestling there as he dug into his pocket and produced a money-clip. He returned the twenty to the clip, extracted a fifty, and dropped it in front of the clerk. The man's eyes shifted from the gun to the new bill lying on the counter. He nervously wet his lips and said, "I really don't see ..."

"I don't want you to see anything," Bolan said pleasantly. "And I don't need to stand here playing games with my bankroll. I *could* just drag

86

you across that desk and slap you silly. You think of that?"

Apparently the thought had crossed the clerk's mind. The words came then in a warmly conspiratorial stream. "The man just wanted to know who you were and what your connections are, Mr. Lambretta. I figured you had nothing to hide. I told him how long you'd been here and what a quiet, cultured man you seem to be. Oh, and I believe I told him that Mrs. D'Agosta had called for you here a time or two. Was I indiscreet? I hope not. Mrs. D'Agosta is such a fine young lady ... certainly too young to be widowed. It's a shame, such a shame."

"And you told him about the ponies."

"Yes sir, I believe I did. Oh, but I'm sure it's quite all right. I have handled bets for this gentleman also."

"So who is he?"

The clerk's lower lip trembled. "A Mr. Marasco. I believe they call him *Honey* Marasco. Odd name for such a burly person, but that's ..."

"And you told him about my mail?"

The clerk's face was becoming contorted with the evidence of an inner conflict becoming apparent. "I ... uh ... Marasco is connected with Julian DiGeorge, Mr. Lambretta. You're aware, certainly, that Mr. DiGeorge is Mrs. D'Agosta's father. So, all things considered, I saw no harm in ... in ..."

"You told him about my mail!"

"Yes sir. I told him that you had received letters from New Jersey and Florida. Was I violating a ..."

Bolan said, "No, no, forget it," and pushed the fifty into the clerk's sweating palm. He was smiling as he crossed the lobby and went out the door. The cover was falling into place.

Chapter Twelve

THIN BLOOD

"This guy is just a cheap hood, *bambina*," Di-George told his daughter. Though he despised the use of old-country phrases in general conversation, the *bambina* was an endearment he used whenever he wished to emphasize the intimate nature of a father-daughter relationship. Andrea understood this bit of family psychology and went along with it. The so-called generation gap was nowhere more evident than in the DiGeorge household. Mother and daughter had long ago lost all semblances of a common ground for unemotional conversation; indeed, Mama was rarely at home these days, preferring to spend most of her golden age on the Italian Riviera. Between father and daughter, *bambina* had become a sort of truce word, with a history reaching back to the aftermath of Andrea's first paddling at the age of three. So, *bambina* had become a place to bury the hatchet, or to gloss over ruffled sensitivities, or to smooth the way for an unpleasant bit of news, which DiGeorge obviously presumed that he was now delivering. "He don't even have any connections," the troubled father continued. "He's a free-lancer, a punk, a two-bit rodman and drifter who's for hire to the world at large. I hate to tell you this, but you got to be careful who you bring into the home, baby. A free-coaster like this could cause all sorts of trouble to your Poppa's business arrangements. Besides, a guy like this is just going to wind up with a bullet in the neck and a weeping widow, and he's liable to take someone with him. Now I'm not trying to say I should pick your friends, but ... well ... listen, *bambina,* you're in the know now, and you know how careful your Poppa has got to be."

"Where did you get all this information?" Andrea asked in a surprisingly casual tone.

"Hey, it's my business to know things."

"Yes, I realize that, Poppa," Andrea said patiently, "but your sources are off the track this time. Frank is a ... a ... well, I don't know how he makes his living and I don't even care. He's first class in my book and that's all I care to know." Her veils came down and she sank her hooks into the tenderest area of her father's psyche. "After all, where would *I* be now if Momma had asked *you* for a character reference 30 years ago?"

"Ah, ah, ah," DiGeorge groaned. He banged his elbow against the wall and worked his fingers into a series of fists. "You're not trying to be reasonable, *bambina,*" he said. "You're just trying to make your Poppa feel like a heel. Okay, okay. I feel like one. But not because of anything I ever did to you or for you. So I've done some things I don't want to strut around and talk about—so any man can say the same. Times have changed now, the world has changed, and there ain't no room in it for two-bit rodmen anymore. Hey, you think your old man hasn't always had his wife and kid's best interests in mind? Huh? You think that?"

"You'd have cut Momma's throat and mine too at the first demand of your blood brothers, and you know that's true," Andrea replied dismally. "Even now you'd do it. 'Our thing' first, last, and always—isn't that the way it is, Poppa? Above family, above state, above God even, loyalty to 'this thing we have'—isn't that right, Poppa?"

Andrea had again struck a raw nerve. The

color had drained from DiGeorge's face when his daughter spoke the phrase "our thing." He laughed nervously and said, "Hey, where are you getting this stuff? These fairy tales you been listening to, eh? Who's been telling my *bambina* these old-country fairy tales?"

"They're not fairy tales, and they're not old-country," Andrea stated flatly. "The vintage is the late twenties or early thirties, and the origin is strictly New York, a long ways from the old country. The whole thing is common knowledge now, Poppa. I wouldn't be surprised if it isn't being taught in American History classes. So who're you trying to kid? You'd better get modern and get with it. The Mafia and the Cosa Nostra are one and the same, the whole world knows it, and you're up to your eyes in it, and I know who you are and *what* you are. So don't come around here giving me the *bambina* routine and trying to tell me that the *daughter* of a common hood is too good to become the *wife* of one. Like mother like daughter, Poppa. You're stuck with us both, so you may as well decide to make the most of it."

Julian DiGeorge was not angry. Nor even hurt, now. He was frightened, and saddened. "Okay, so you wanted to hurt the old man and you've hurt him," he said quietly. "Okay, I guess I don't blame you. And I guess I'm glad it's out in the open now, so I can see the claws coming before they scratch. You're a hundred percent right, *bambina*. Deej was a nothing until the brotherhood came along and made him a somebody. You're right. I got no fancy schooling like you did, and I didn't grow up with roasted pheasants for breakfast neither."

He raised his arms to shoulder level and gazed

around the luxurious surroundings as though perhaps seeing them for the first time ever. "As for a place like this—when Deej was a kid, a place like this was strictly from fairy tales. Everything you got, remember this, you owe to *this thing* of ours. The *Cosa Nostra*, yeah, it gave you the clothes on your back and the food in your belly and yeah, your old man is loyal to a thing like this and if you had any sense, you'd be too instead of smart-mouthing it. And you better remember this, smart-mouth, you ain't so wrong as to just be digging your Poppa with emptiness. What you said was right, about throats getting cut and such. It could happen to anybody, even to a *Capo's bambina*. Eh? You thought I'd deny it? Well, Deej is *not* denying it. If I was a Miss Smart Mouth, I think I'd be damn careful where my words were going and what they was saying about my Poppa's friends. Huh? Deej is big, sure, the biggest thing west of Phoenix, but not as big as God, *bambina*. When an order comes down from the top, it comes down, and a hit is a hit, and it don't ask whose daughter is this or whose wife is this."

DiGeorge got to his feet and stared at his daughter with forlorn eyes. "This is a rotten conversation for a father and his kid. There isn't going to be no more like this."

"No, Poppa, there won't be any more," Andrea replied quietly.

"You'll tell this Lambretta punk to get lost."

She sighed. "Yes, Poppa. He's coming to dinner. I'll tell him then."

"You want me to tell 'im?" DiGeorge asked gently.

"Yes. Yes, I guess so." Her eyes suddenly brimming with tears, the girl jumped to her feet and cried, "I'm *sorry*, Poppa," and ran out of the room.

"I'm sorry too, *bambina*," DiGeorge told the empty room. He picked up a heavy glass ashtray and hurled it against the far wall.

Chapter Thirteen

CHARISMA

Bolan was shown into the DiGeorge library by a steely-eyed "butler" in formal attire which almost but not quite concealed a gun under the left arm. He was offered a drink, accepted a fancy tumbler of Scotch on the rocks, and was asked to make himself comfortable. He did so, dropping into a heavy leather lounge. A pedestal-type ashtray immediately appeared at his right elbow; the butler excused himself and departed. The lighting was dim and the dark panelling of the room seemed to cast ominous shadows across Bolan's view. His eyes were roving the bookshelves, seeing while not seeing the obviously never disturbed volumes reposing there. A chill trickled down his neck to the base of his spine; he was, he knew, being watched from some concealed observation post. He casually lit a cigarette then got to his feet and paced about the room gulping the Scotch on the move.

Bolan placed the empty glass on a desk, opened his coat, inspected his gunleather in an obvious manner, closed his coat, and paced some more. Presently the door opened and two men entered. One of them Bolan recognized as an obscure palace guard, a smooth-faced youngster who could have just stepped off an Ivy League campus. The other was a very light-stepping heavyweight with a ground-beef face, massive shoulders, and ridiculously small feet. It was the same man Bolan had encountered earlier in the parking lot. The youth halted just inside the doorway and allowed Bolan to see his .38—the older man stood an arm's reach from Bolan's gun hand.

"You forgot to check your hardware," said little-feet, pleasantly enough.

"I like to know who I'm checking it with," Bolan replied stiffly.

"The name's Marasco," the heavyweight solemnly told him.

Bolan nodded. "Okay," he said. His hand moved slowly to the coatfront.

Marasco said quickly, "Not that way. Lean over, both hands on the desk."

"Huh-uh," Bolan replied, grinning. His eyes flashed in a quick round trip to the youth at the door. "I don't turn my back to no rodman."

"Slow and easy, then," Marasco said, almost smiling. "Lay it on the desk."

Bolan complied with the instructions. Marasco stepped forward, took the pistol, and casually dropped it into his coat pocket. "You can pick it up at the gate on your way out," he said lightly. He took one step toward the door, then paused and turned back to Bolan as though in an afterthought. "Your name Lambretta?"

Bolan nodded a silent affirmation.

"You connected with a Rocky Lambretta from Jersey City?"

"Rocky was a cousin," Bolan replied unemotionally. "He's been dead since '62."

Marasco jerked his head in an understanding nod, took another step toward the door, paused and turned back again. "*Frankie*, is it?"

Bolan grinned and said, "Why the twenty questions? You know my name."

"You ever work in Miami or Saint Pete?"

"You want me to sit down and write you out a life history?"

Marasco shrugged his shoulders and went on to

the door. "Mr. DiGeorge will be down in a minute," he said. "Just make yourself at home."

"I was comfortable before you came in here," Bolan said sarcastically.

Marasco winked and made his exit. The youth grinned at Bolan and followed the heavier man out, pulling the door closed. Bolan kept his face expressionless and stared at the closed door for a long moment, then went over to the sideboard and poured himself another drink. He still felt eyes upon him, but had no fears that he could not behave in a convincing manner. He had grown up in an Italian neighborhood; as for understanding the enemy, his brief apprenticeship with the Sergio Frenchi family in the opening days of the Pittsfield adventure would prove of inestimable value in the days which lay ahead. Bolan continued to play the role, gulping the Scotch while restlessly pacing about the room. Five minutes later, Julian DiGeorge made his appearance.

Without preliminaries, he asked, "What're you doing in the Springs?"

Bolan said, "Look, to hell with it. It was just a gag I went along with. I never had no serious eyes on your kid. We had a few laughs and that was it. You walked in on us and I was just trying to save the kid some face. But enough's enough."

"Answer my question," DiGeorge demanded. His face had not changed expression.

"You already got the answers!" Bolan exploded.

"Why were you fooling around with my daughter?"

Bolan bugged his eyes and said, "You kidding? What man wouldn't go for ..." He abruptly stopped talking, dug in his pocket for a cigarette, stuck it between his lips then pulled it away without lighting it. "Look, Deej, the girl's of age,

97

she's a beauty, and she ain't exactly no Virgin Mary if you'll pardon the comparison. We met in the bar at my hotel, and we laughed around a little, and we got to be friends. No one could be more surprised than me when I find out later whose kid she turns out to be. Her name's D'Agosta, you know, not DiGeorge anymore. Hell, I didn't know who she was. We only met three days ago."

DiGeorge's shoulders had tightened noticeably but his face remained impassive. "What brought you to the Springs?" he demanded quietly.

Bolan whipped a large, folded news clipping from his pocket and slapped it on the desk. "Need you really ask?" he said disgustedly.

DiGeorge stepped to the desk and picked up the clipping, unfolded it, glanced at it, then dropped it with a chuckle. "It figures," he said.

Bolan picked up his clipping, a news story concerning the Executioner's Los Angeles exploits, a large close-up photo of Bolan's face dominating the item. "The word's that the contract is wide open," Bolan muttered past his Lambretta mask.

"And you thought you'd pick up a quick'n easy hundred thou," the Mafia boss said, still chuckling.

"I got it that you had a dugout here. I figured it was worth a play."

"Did you also get it that this Bolan punk is probably in Brazil by now? Or better yet, that he's dead and buried in a secret grave by the cops up at the Village?"

Bolan snorted and said, "He's right here in Palm Springs!"

DiGeorge's amused expression immediately evaporated. "Where did you get that?"

"We already tangled once." Bolan quickly unbuttoned his shirt, spread it wide, and displayed a quarter-inch-wide groove in the flesh just beneath his left armpit. "A .45 slug dug that trench, and it had the Executioner's brand on it."

"Don't say that word!" DiGeorge snapped.

"What word?"

"Don't call the punk by his pet name! Lemme see that scratch!"

"Scratch, hell," Bolan said. He adjusted the shirt to afford DiGeorge a better inspection of the wound.

DiGeorge clucked his tongue and said, "You were lucky, Franky. Another inch to the right, and you ..." He let go the shirt and studied the wound with an academic air. "It's healing pretty good. What is it—about a week old?"

"About that," Bolan said. He rebuttoned the shirt and carefully tucked in the tails.

"Yeah, you were lucky," DiGeorge repeated. "Franky Lucky, that's a name that ought to stick. Not many guys walking around can talk about their gunfight with this Bolan. You sure that was him?"

A new air of respect had pervaded the previously strained atmosphere between the two men. Bolan recognized it immediately. "It was him all right," he replied. "We came up eyeball to eyeball down by Desert Junction last Tuesday night."

"That's only a half a mile from here," DiGeorge uneasily noted.

"Yeah. I was coming up to lay out this place. I guess he was too. We laid out each other instead."

"You hit 'im?" DiGeorge quickly asked.

"I don't think so. It came up too quick, too unexpected you know. We're side by side, at this stoplight, see. I see him, and he sees me seeing him, and then we're banging away at each other. There's lights coming down from your place. He

99

whips his car around and takes off. I figure there'll be another time, and I don't want to go off on no running gun battle through the city. Besides, I'm hit, see."

"What kind of car was he in, Lucky?"

"Big job . . . Chrysler, I think."

"Uh huh." DiGeorge smacked his palms together and paced an erratic circle around the desk. "This was a week ago Tuesday night?"

"Yeah. But I'd take book he's still around."

DiGeorge raised a fist to his mouth and nibbled a heavy knuckle. "Maybe you hit 'im," he said. "Maybe that's why he's laying low."

"Maybe."

The conversation was interrupted by the noisy appearance of Andrea D'Agosta. She swept into the room with a small overnight bag dangling from one hand, viciously banged the door, and dropped the bag to the floor. "Did you tell the punk to get lost yet, Poppa?" she asked loudly.

"Not yet," DiGeorge growled, eyeing her unapprovingly. She wore a glittering mini-sheath with thigh-revealing slits up each leg.

"Well, hurry up!" the girl commanded. "I'm getting lost *with* him, and I can't get out of this nuthouse fast enough." Her eyes rested on Bolan. "Come on, Frank, let's split."

"You're going *nowhere*," DiGeorge told her. "You're staying *put!*"

"Or you'll shoot me if I leave, and you'll cut my throat if I stay." She laughed shrilly and went over to put a hand on Bolan's arm. "How about that, Frank?" she giggled. "What do you think of a man who threatens his own daughter with a Mafia-style rubout? Isn't that the dying end?" From somewhere a small nickel-plated .22 had appeared in her hand. "Come on, Frank. I'll shoot our way out of this joint." She laughed even more

100

shrilly and said, "Don't look so shocked, Poppa. It's in my blood, see. Like father, like daughter. I was born with a right to kill."

DiGeorge had the look of a man who could just lie down and die. Bolan twisted the little gun out of the girl's hand in almost the same motion as he hit her with the flat of his other hand. She staggered across the floor and sank to her knees, the angry red handprint standing out starkly from a bloodless background. "Well, for God's sake," she murmured in a dazed voice.

Bolan dropped the gun onto the desk, crossed to the girl, tenderly kissed the handprint on her cheek, and tossed her across his shoulder. "Where does she belong?" he quietly asked DiGeorge.

"First room up the stairs," DiGeorge mumbled woodenly. He followed Bolan to the hallway, where they were met by an obviously uncomfortable Honey Marasco.

"For God's sake," Andrea repeated weakly, her head and torso inverted down Bolan's back.

"Drunk as a skunk," Bolan told Marasco with a grin. He stepped around the bodyguard and started up the stairs.

DiGeorge headed up with him, then paused at the first step and turned back to Marasco. "Oh, this is Frank Lucky, Phil. He's coming with us. Right, Franky?"

"Right," Bolan replied without turning around. *Lucky* was right, he was thinking. Lucky that Julian DiGeorge could not tell the difference between a week-old and a two-week-old wound. Lucky that Bolan always seemed to be at the right spot at precisely the right time. And luckier than all, perhaps, for so much dissension in the DiGeorge household. He carried the girl into her room and gently placed her on the bed.

DiGeorge sat down beside her and said,

"Thanks, Franky. I'll stay with her awhile. We got some things to talk out, me'n her. You go on downstairs and get acquainted. And, later on, you'n me have some things to talk out."

"I'll be looking forward to that," the Executioner assured the *Capo*. And then Franky Lucky Bolan went downstairs and joined the family.

Chapter Fourteen

THE POINTER

Carl Lyons, released from the Hardcase Detail upon his return from Palm Village, had immediately taken a ten-day vacation, most of which he spent with his wife and young son on a carefree motor trip along the Baja California peninsula. He had returned to duty on October 20th, tanned and rested and eagerly wondering about the nature of his new assignment. The life and fortunes of one Mack Bolan had been insistently tamped into the lower reaches of his mind. He hoped he could keep the maverick down there. Carl Lyons had always been a "good cop." He wanted to go on being one. He did not want Mack Bolan back inside his official life. With some perverse persistency of fate, however, Bolan was destined to get there again just the same.

The most interesting scuttlebutt in the bullrooms all had to do with the demise of Hardcase and the uncertain future of Big Tim Braddock. This information saddened Lyons; he had a great respect for the hard-boiled Detective Captain, if not outright affection. Lyons was, of course, in no small measure responsible for Braddock's failure to apprehend the Executioner. This was a sore point to his conscience and a constant irritant to his sense of duty and loyalty; still, Lyons continued his silent argument that even a cop's first duty was to his own sense of personal ethics. In this context of understanding, he had pursued the only course open to him in his handling of the Bolan case. Twice he had turned his back and allowed the Executioner to walk away from him.

103

Braddock had never known of this treachery, of course, and Lyons himself simply could not regard his actions as treacherous. The life of one damn good man had hung in the balance, and even Big Tim Braddock and his ambitions had been outweighed on the scales of Lyons' ethics.

In every sense, then, Lyons was happy to be off Hardcase. He hoped never to see or hear of Mack Bolan again. He picked up his assignment, a nightwatch in Vice, and went up to check in with his new lieutenant. Lyons was welcomed to the squad, they chatted briefly, then the young Sergeant went into the bullroom with a stack of directives and memorandums which required his reading. At shortly past midnight, while still poring through the bulletins, his new partner, Patrolman Al Macintosh, informed Lyons that he was wanted on the telephone. "Switchboard says it's an eyes-call," Macintosh added.

"I don't know any Vice informants, Al," Lyons replied, glaring ruefully at the imposing pile of reading matter. "Why don't you take it."

"Guy asked for you personally, Carl," the Patrolman reported.

Lyons raised his eyebrows in surprise, scooped up the phone, and said, "Sergeant Lyons here."

"This is long distance so let's keep it brief," a muffled voice responded. "I want you to set me up with a federal narcotics agent. I have some information they'd like to have."

"Why me?" Lyons asked. "Where'd you get my name?"

"Reliable source," the voice replied. "I can't be too careful. Neither can you. Will you set it up?"

"I can try," Lyons said. He signalled quietly to Macintosh. The other officer went into the next room and lifted an extension telephone on the same line. "Give me your name and number," Lyons requested, "and I'll get back with you as soon as possible."

"You know better than that," the caller said, chuckling. "Can I get you at this same number at five this morning?"

"I'll try to arrange it," the Sergeant replied. "I can't promise anything."

"You try. Get me a name and number I can unload this info to, and make sure it's straight. This is hot, very hot, and it can't wait too long."

"Why don't you just unload it on me?" Lyons suggested. Macintosh, staring at him through the open doorway, gave Lyons a wink.

The caller hesitated shortly, then: "I don't think you want to get involved in this."

"I can pass along anything you have to the proper person," Lyons assured him.

"This has to do with a narcotics smuggling ring. It's Mafia, Lyons, and it's big, *damn* big. I've got names, dates, and routes, bills of lading, all kinds of junk. It's too much for a telephone contact. And I don't want any middle men."

"I'll meet you someplace," Lyons suggested, smiling across the open space at his partner.

"You're sure you want in this?"

"It's my job, Mister . . . Mister . . ."

"Why don't you just call me Pointer. You be thinking it over. I'll call back at five to complete the set. Don't mess it up, now."

A sudden and stunning suspicion jolted the Sergeant. "This isn't *Bolan*, is it?" he asked.

Without a pause the reply came, "Word has it that Bolan is dead."

"Oh?"

"I'll call at five."

"Let me see if I have this straight," Lyons said hurriedly. "Are you *inside* the Mafia, Pointer?"

"I sure am."

The connection was then broken. Macintosh replaced his instrument and quickly rejoined Lyons. "This could be the biggest thing since Valachi," the young Patrolman commented excitedly.

"I'm just glad you heard it," Lyons replied. He pushed aside the stack of reading matter and scraped his chair back. "Let's go tell the Lieutenant. Pointer said he was calling long distance. I wonder how long a distance. I wonder where he got my name. I wonder what the hell his angle is."

Wonders would never cease, as Sgt. Lyons was to discover shortly. A few hours later, Big Tim Braddock would draw his new assignment also. The life and fortunes of Mack Bolan, who was very much alive and well in Palm Springs, were beginning a new weaving which would involve them all in a new and violent tapestry of terror.

At 7:30 on the morning of October 21st, a new and highly secret undercover detail was launched at the L.A. Hall of Justice. Code-named Pointer, the operation was the ultimate in inter-agency cooperation and was staffed by Carl Lyons and Al Macintosh of LAPD; Harold Brognola of the U.S. Department of Justice, Racketeering Investigative Group; Raymond Portoccesi of the Los Angeles FBI Office; and U.S. Treasury Narcotics Agents George Bruemeyer and Manuel de Laveirca.

Mack Bolan's Lambretta mask was opening the Mafia doors to the fresh air of law enforcement, and the Executioner's unrelenting war on the giant crime syndicate was entering a dramatic and suspenseful new phase. As the various threads of the weave began coming together, pain and terror and violence and wholesale slaughter would stalk that gray no man's landscape separating the just from the unjust, Mack Bolan's definition of *hell*.

Chapter Fifteen

INQUEST

Willie Walker and his crew had returned some days earlier with a completely negative report concerning the status and whereabouts of both Mack Bolan and Lou Pena. "That town is clean as a whistle, Deej," Walker reported. "If they've got this Bolan buried up there, nobody knows it. We pumped everybody from the Mayor to the gravediggers. As for Screwy Looey, he ain't left no tracks nowhere. If you would ask me, I'll have to say it looks like Looey is layin' low. Or else this Bolan got to him and left 'im in a shallow grave somewhere."

Walker and his crew were returned to a red-alert status and diffused into Palm Springs environs in a quiet but continuous patrol operation. All important visitors arriving at the DiGeorge country estate, of which there had been an unusual number in recent days, were convoyed from and to the airport by strong security crews, and the villa itself was a veritable armed camp. Andrea D'Agosta was under virtual house-arrest and was rarely seen about the grounds; on occasional brief visits to the family swimming pool, she had been closely escorted by several watchful members of the palace guard.

Tensions had seemed to grow rather than to dissipate and by the 21st day of October, Julian DiGeorge's uneasiness had reached an intolerable level. He summoned Philip Honey Marasco to his chambers in the early afternoon and told the burly bodyguard, "I'm getting a nervous feeling about Screwy Looey. I wonder if you could find somebody to get in touch with him."

His face an impassive mask, Marasco replied, "Looey should know better than to worry you this way, Deej. He shouldn't make you go looking for him."

"You're thinking like me," DiGeorge said. "We know what's what, Phil. Screwy Looey is laying low on me."

"A guy shouldn't be afraid of his own family," Marasco commented. "I think it's his pride, maybe. He told some of the boys he wasn't coming back without this Bolan's head."

"Somebody," DiGeorge said thoughtfully, "ought to put the word out that Screwy Looey had better get back home."

Marasco thoroughly understood the tone of this genteel conversation. To an outsider, DiGeorge's complaint might have sounded like nothing more than idle fretting. In the language of the Family, however, the message was as clear as a military command. Marasco jerked his head in a casual nod and replied, "I'll put the word out, Deej. Is there anything special you want said to Looey?"

DiGeorge studied his fingertips and said, "In this thing of ours, Philip Honey, we either stand together or we die alone."

Marasco briefly drummed his fingers on DiGeorge's desk, then said, "Yeah," and turned to leave.

"What are you making on Franky Lucky?" DiGeorge asked casually.

Emotion entered Marasco's features for the first time during the interview. He turned back to his boss with a heavy frown. "Everything checks, Deej, but hell, I just don't know. All the boys like 'im. He's tough and hard as a rock, but he don't go throwing his weight around. It ain't like he's

108

trying to make up to everybody, you know ... I mean, he don't step away from trouble, he just don't go looking for any. And the boys like 'im, I mean like they kind of look up to 'im, you know ... But I just ... don't ..."

"Yeah. I know what you mean, Phil. Something bothers me, too, and I just can't finger it. You're sure his history checks out, eh?"

Marasco's frown deepened. "Yeah, it all checks. He don't leave many tracks, though. I guess he's been pretty much of a loner. But I finally got a line on a guy that knew 'im out in Jersey. The guy's in jail down in Florida, though."

"You know what to do about that," DiGeorge said quietly.

"Yeah. I already started the routine to spring 'im, but it does take some time, you know. Meanwhile I sent Victor Poppy down. He'll make the conversation and he ought to be back tomorrow sometime. Then maybe we'll know just how lucky this Franky Lucky really is."

"You know, I hope this boy checks out," DiGeorge said, sighing.

"So do I," Marasco replied.

"Meanwhile you watch 'im."

"Sure, Deej."

"We're going to have to open the family up some, you know. I'm going to take it up with the *Commissione.* And I'd like to sponsor this Franky Lucky. I just hope he checks out."

Marasco turned away again. He paused with a hand on the door and said, "He's got his own ideas. I'm letting him run around all he wants to outside. If this Bolan *is* still around, I'm betting Franky Lucky is the boy to come up with him."

"Yeah, yeah," DiGeorge said tiredly. "And don't forget about Screwy Looey."

"I'll have the word out in ten minutes, Deej."

"You know what I want, Phil."

"I know what you want, Deej."

In such simple and seemingly casual terms were the preliminaries established for a Mafia murder contract. Screwy Looey Pena was behaving irrationally, to DiGeorge's thinking. Irrational behavior, went that thinking, was usually indicative of a guilty conscience. *Capo* Julian DiGeorge was intensely curious as to the reasons behind Lou Pena's continued avoidance of the family home. He would either have those reasons within the next 24 hours, or a murder contract, or both. Philip Honey Marasco, at that moment, knew precisely what his *Capo* wanted.

Thirty minutes later, no one at the DiGeorge villa knew precisely what anyone wanted. The electrifying news that rattled the family group arrived by way of a breathless "runner" who was brought to the villa in a chartered helicopter. The messenger, a "soldier" in Tony Danger's crew, received an immediate audience with the *Capo* and excitedly told him, "They busted us wide open, Mr. DiGeorge. I mean everywhere. They knocked . . ."

"Waitaminnit, waitaminnit!" DiGeorge growled. "They *who?*"

"Federals, I guess. They knocked over our warehouse in Chula Vista and picked off all the stuff, even the stuff under the floors. Tony Danger wasn't a block away, he just got away in time. He says to tell you the Mexicans picked up Morales just after he got off the stockpile shipment. He's try'na get word to the boats, but he ain't so sure it ain't too late for that."

DiGeorge passed a weary hand over his eyes and muttered, "What about the boats? What about 'em?"

"I don't know what about 'em, Mr. DiGeorge.

110

Neither does Tony. That's what I meant. Tony don't know . . ."

"Tony don't know if his ass is on or off," Di-George snapped. "I mean how much of the stuff is on the boats?"

"Oh, well the whole stockpile, Mr. DiGeorge. That's what I . . ."

"Where is Tony Danger now?"

"He went down to the port to . . ."

"Then he's a damn dumb bastard!" DiGeorge growled. "If they know everything else, then they know about the port, too. He probably walked right into 'em. Okay. So we got a rat somewhere in the woodpile. You get in that whirlybird and get on back down to San Diego. If you find Tony Danger you tell him Deej says to kill everything, I mean all of it, everything stops. And you tell him that Deej personally wants the rat, so don't go taking nothing on himself. Now you go on. On your way out, tell Willie Walker and Philip Honey I want 'em in here right now."

Some minutes later, while the villa seethed with excitement, DiGeorge confided to Walker and Marasco. "I've just had this feeling. Something has been wrong, and I knew it. Now I guess I know *what*. I'm thinking about two names right now. You know the names I'm thinkin' of?"

"Screwy Looey," Marasco quietly replied.

"Franky Lucky," said Walker.

"Okay, but let's not jump too fast," DiGeorge cautioned them. His gaze fell speculatively on Marasco. "See if you can raise Victor Poppy and see if he's got any news for us. Let's see how lucky Franky Lucky is."

Marasco nodded his head solemnly and went to the telephone.

"Start the juice going," DiGeorge told Willie Walker. "Any place Screwy Looey could have lit

111

down. Get into our connections uptown, gather up whatever crumbs you can find about this rumble, and see what can be put together."

Walker curtly nodded his head and departed. Marasco was direct-dialing an area code in Florida, reading the number from a pocket-sized spiral notebook. He completed the dialing and turned about to gaze at DiGeorge as the connection was being made. The conversation was brief, with Marasco doing most of the listening. Then he hung up and released an almost sad sigh.

"Okay," DiGeorge said impatiently, "what's the bad news?"

"Victor Poppy says this guy hasn't seen Frank Lucky in over five years. The guy says the last he heard, Franky Lucky had got drafted and got it in Vietnam."

"Got what?" DiGeorge asked tensely.

"Killed, Deej."

The room became very quiet. After a moment, DiGeorge said, "The guy in Florida could have heard wrong."

"It's like hearsay evidence," Marasco agreed.

"We got to give this Franky Lucky a chance to clear it up for us."

"I hope he can, Deej."

DiGeorge released a long sigh. "So do I. You let me handle it. When is Victor getting back with this Florida boy?"

"He says he already oiled the wheels and they're turning pretty fast. He hopes maybe tomorrow. Maybe even sooner."

"Okay. You tell Franky Lucky I wanta talk to 'im, eh Phil?"

Marasco said, "Soon as he gets back."

"Where'd he go?"

Marasco shrugged his shoulders. "I told you, he's got his own ideas about things."

"Maybe his ideas are too big, Phil."

"Could be. He's been here just about all day though, Deej. Left about an hour ago. I can't hardly buy this boy as an informer, I just can't hardly believe it."

"Aaah hell, Phil," DiGeorge said miserably, "I've been making plans about sponsoring this boy. You know that. I like 'im, too. But I don't like *any* boy *that* well, and you know that too."

"I know that, Deej."

"You better get something ready, just in case."

"I'll have it ready, Deej. And I'll send him in as soon as he gets back."

"You do that." DiGeorge spun his chair about and stared glumly out the window. Several of his armed "soldiers" could be seen strolling the grounds. "Yeah, Phil, you do that."

Chapter Sixteen

THE CONTRACT

Carl Lyons arrived in the city of Redlands, just east of Los Angeles, shortly after dark on the evening of October 21st. He proceeded directly to a drive-in theatre and parked in the second row behind the concession building. Following instructions received earlier, he left the vehicle immediately, went to the snack bar, and purchased a candy bar and a box of popcorn. Moments later he returned to his car, a rear door on the passenger side opened and a man slid into the seat behind him. Lyons continued staring toward the screen and said, "Mr. Pointer?"

"That's me," the man said. "How did it go?"

"You were right on target, Pointer," Lyons replied. "We netted 20 kilos of H and about a ton of pot."

"They've been bunching it up, scared to move it with all the attention at the border crossings," Bolan-Pointer commented, chuckling.

"The best part," Lyons added, "is that we took out their entire supply line, from the Mexican side all the way."

"That was just the acquisition route," Bolan told him. "I have details here of one of their distribution set-ups. I'm leaving it on the back seat."

"I'm going to turn around," Lyons announced casually.

Bolan lit a cigarette and said, "Okay. But you won't see anything."

The police sergeant swivelled about with one arm on the back rest and peered into the darkness of the rear corner. He made out only a

115

lean figure in a lightweight suit, a felt hat pulled low over the forehead. "We'd like to have your name," he said faintly.

"You'd better be satisfied with what you're getting," Bolan replied. "You know a town called Blythe?"

"Sure, it's just this side of the Arizona border." The policeman was still trying to make an identification. He noted that his informant wore tight-fitting suede gloves. The cigarette glowed faintly as the man took a heavy drag, allowing Lyons to see enough to produce a curious feeling of letdown. "I guess I've been halfway thinking that you were Bolan," he said.

"And now?"

"Well I know you're not Bolan. The voice is close enough, but not the face. Okay, Pointer. What about Blythe?"

"It's in the package I'm leaving you. There's an old B-17 base near there. It was closed down right after World War Two. Being used now as a public airport, but very little traffic. A lieutenant by the name of Gagliano is running the operation there, in an old building that used to be a hangar. It's a powder plant."

"A what?"

"It's where they cut the H, dilute it down, and package it. Then they wholesale it out from that point. Deliveries are made in small, private airplanes. The wholesale end of it is all done by air. I don't have any poop on the retail lines, and I gather that the organization isn't even working that end of it."

"How's the market?"

"Frantic, since the border pressure. The stuff's been stockpiling on the Mexican side, retail outlets are flipping for buys."

"Price should be good, then," he said.

Bolan grunted. "They're buying uncut H at a little over two thousand per kilo, then whole-saling the cut stuff at a going price that has lately gone to 14 thou the kilo."

Lyons whistled softly. "The profits in junk," he commented in an awed tone.

"Yeah. I wouldn't recommend moving on Blythe right away. They'll be cooling it after your hit this morning."

"We let one of their boats get through," Lyons said. "We're watching it."

"Good thinking. Play it right and you can line up their entire wholesaling operation."

"You know," Lyons said thoughtfully, "you *could* be Bolan."

His guest laughed and replied, "You just won't let it go, will you?"

"You think like him and you talk like him and it wouldn't take too damn much to make you *look* like him."

Bolan laughed again and replied, "The word's all around that the guy got it at Palm Village."

"We've never found a body. Just how much do you know about Palm Village, Pointer?"

"An old gunner by the name of Pena was in charge up there. Somehow he's missing in action, or something. The whole mob is wondering about him."

"Pena is in custody," Lyons said.

"Yeah?"

"You interested?"

"I guess I am. Fair exchange?"

"No reason not to tell you," Lyons said. "The news is probably out by now, anyway, or will be. Braddock went up there today and busted the thing wide open."

"What do you mean? What thing?"

"The Palm Village police have had Pena under

117

protective custody since shortly after the fire-works up there. His own request, as I understand it." Lyons laughed. "That head cop up there is something else. He's been hiding Pena in his own home. No charges, no nothing—just sanctuary. Or that was the way Braddock read it." The po-liceman's eyelids dropped to a half closure and he added, "Aren't you going to ask me who Brad-dock is?"

"I know who Braddock is," Bolan replied coolly.

"I know who you are, too," the Sergeant said. "You're Mack Bolan."

"You're out of your mind," Bolan said, laugh-ing.

"It's a good face job, Bolan. I had no idea it could be done so quickly. What's your cover? Maybe I can help you strengthen it."

"Thanks, but you're still out of your mind." Bolan cracked the door and Lyons got a good look at the face as the interior light flashed on. "I'll give you a call for the next setup."

"Do that," Lyons murmured. "One of the people in this detail would be interested in any-thing you might learn about the Palm Village massacre. He'd appreciate some intelligence, asked me to tell you that."

"Who's the interested party?"

"Agent named Brognola, Justice Department. He's interested in rackets."

"Everybody's interested in rackets these days," Bolan said. "Brognola, huh? I'm not sure I like the name."

"Hell, he's straight. Just because his name sounds Italian, you can't . . ."

"I know, I know," Bolan protested, chuckling. "Some of my best friends have Italian names."

He got out of the car and walked into the darkness.

Julian DiGeorge stepped forward to greet Franky Lucky with a wide grin and a warm clasp of arms. "Come on in, siddown, siddown," the *Capo* said. "I was just fixin' some drinks. You still with Scotch?"

Franky Lucky Bolan smiled tiredly and dropped into a chair. "Sure, that's great, Deej," he replied. Philip Marasco leaned over to light Bolan's cigarette. DiGeorge thrust a glass of Scotch and ice into his hand and settled into the other chair. They sat in a sort of triangular arrangement, with Bolan at the point. The implications of the overly warm hospitality were not lost on Bolan. He realized that a lot of effort was being exerted to put him at ease. Outwardly, it worked—but his mind was seething with the possibilities of directions which the interview could take.

"You're looking tired, Franky," DiGeorge observed. "You're sure a go-getter. I guess you don't hardly stop all day long, eh?"

"It's not that bad," Bolan said. "I'm used to depending all on myself. I'll get used to an organization around me pretty soon."

"Feel like you're getting any closer to this Bolan?" Marasco asked quietly.

"Yeah and something else, too," Bolan replied quickly, staring steadily at the bodyguard. "What's this I hear about the big Mexican bust?"

"Just one of those things, Franky," DiGeorge put in hurriedly. "We learn to roll with the punches. Forget it. Hey, you always worked alone, eh? You never were in the army or navy or anything?"

Bolan snickered and flashed a broad grin to

119

Marasco. "Hey, Philip Honey, does the boss think I'm that big a sucker?"

DiGeorge chuckled and hid his eyes in his glass. He sipped the drink, then came back with, "Only suckers put on the uniform, eh? Did you burn your draft card, Lucky?"

"Only suckers burn their draft cards too," Bolan said genially. "There's better ways. Some guys I heard of even bought themselves a stand-in."

DiGeorge's eyebrows elevated and his eyes locked with Marasco's. "Yeah, I guess I've heard of something like that myself," he said thoughtfully.

"They're not getting no uniform on Franky Lambretta," Bolan said tightly. "Behind a uniform, behind bars, it's all the same. No, thanks." He waved his hand as though to dismiss the entire subject, saying, "Listen, Deej, I stumbled onto something today maybe you should know about. Especially since the big Mexican bust everybody's talking about."

"Yeah?" DiGeorge was smiling archly at Marasco. His gaze flicked to Bolan. "Where you been all day, Lucky?"

"That's what I'm talking about. Listen. I was up around Palm Village. Now I've heard the boys talking about this Screwy Looey Pena. Listen. I think the guy is a bird in a gilded cage."

Marasco's hand jerked toward his pocket and emerged with a pack of cigarettes. DiGeorge exhaled sharply and said, "What're you onto, Lucky?"

"Just this. Screwy Looey has been cozying it up with the cops at Palm Village. All this time. And get this. There's no charges on him, nothin'. I make it that he *asked* to be held."

Marasco's cigarette broke in half and fell to the

120

carpet. He hastily retrieved it and tossed it into an ashtray. "Jesus!" he said.

"What was I telling you, Phil," DiGeorge said softly. "Wasn't I telling you just a few hours ago that someone needs to talk to Screwy Lou?"

"What made him fall apart?" Marasco asked.

"The question is, who puts him back together again?" DiGeorge said.

"You want him put back together, Deej?" Bolan asked casually.

DiGeorge glanced at Marasco and said, "That is exactly what I want, Franky Lucky."

"I work better by myself," Bolan said.

"I like the way you work, Lucky."

Bolan got to his feet and carefully set the empty glass on a table. "Thanks," he said. "Also I see better in the early morning."

"A man should pick his own time and place for his work," DiGeorge said.

"I better get some sleep. I'm dead on my feet."

"Yeah, you do that." DiGeorge stared somberly at Philip Marasco. "You keep on working like this, Lucky, you're gonna wind up with a sponsor. What do you think of that?"

"I think that's great," replied Franky Lucky Bolan. He excused himself and went out.

DiGeorge and Marasco sat in silence for several minutes. Finally Marasco said, "Well?"

"It figures, that's clear enough," DiGeorge said. "He's the kind of guy would hire himself a stand-in."

"He's the kind of guy who's going to be a *Capo* some day," Marasco observed. He smiled. "You better watch out, Deej."

"That's part of the job, isn't it?" DiGeorge puffed. "I gotta leave an heir, don't I? Let's be realistic, Phil, this isn't saying anything against

121

you, but who've I got to turn things over to now, huh? Who've I got?"

"You sure don't have *me*, Deej," Marasco admitted.

"Tell the boys to light a candle for Looey, eh?"

"Sure, Deej."

"I wonder," DiGeorge said thoughtfully, in a barely audible voice, "I just wonder ... you think Frank Lucky's still big with Andrea?"

Marasco grinned. "You thinking of more than one kind of sponsorship, Deej?"

"Maybe. Yeah, maybe. Now wouldn't that be the all of it!"

Chapter Seventeen

MAN ON ICE

Tim Braddock leaned forward in his chair and said, "I just don't see how you could let yourself into a mess like this one, Genghis."

Conn coolly replied, "I wasn't in a mess, Braddock, until you horned in. I had the man on ice, he wasn't bothering anybody, and he was beginning to come around. Now you've got him scared to death again, and he's insisting that I charge him or let him go." The lanky lawman spat wet tobacco leaves on the floor at his feet and added, "I don't see any warrant in *your* hand, Tim."

"We're getting one," Braddock assured his host.

"On *what?*" Conn asked disgustedly.

"You name it, we've got it. Criminal conspiracy, for one. And then everything from intimidation to Murder One."

"In what town were all these crimes perpetrated, Braddock?"

The Captain from Los Angeles smiled serenely. "The conspiracy was originally hatched in Los Angeles and we can prove that. The execution of the crime, or crimes, covered a three-county area and possibly four. Sacramento is working with us on this one. We're going to bust the syndicate in this state, Genghis, with or without the help of hick ... of small-town cops."

"I was told that Hardcase was cancelled," Conn said quietly.

"That's right. And now I'm on special to the Attorney General's office. We're starting here, Genghis, right here in your nice, balanced town.

And you'd better get ready to explain why you've been harboring a known criminal in this balanced little town of yours."

"Who says he's a known criminal?" Conn wanted to know.

"Don't quibble with me over semantics."

The Palm Village Chief pushed his hat back and scratched his forehead. "There's not one shred of anything to link Pena with the hell that hit this town, and you know it. Don't think for a minute that I wouldn't have him booked and walking toward the grand jury if there was. The fact is, Braddock, I have a guest in my home who may or may not be a member of this syndicate you mentioned." Conn stood up suddenly and threw his hat to the floor. "Aw shit, enough of this pussyfooting, Braddock! Let's talk like men!"

Braddock grinned and sailed his own hat across the room. "Let's do that," he replied.

"This Pena character is scared clear out of his skin. He fumbled an assignment, and worse than that, he knows damn well he isn't *ever* going to have the stuff to get the measure of a man like Mack Bolan. He's scared, he's proud, he's getting old and knows it, and he don't want to go home in disgrace. Now that's the way it's laid out. I could like the guy. I could really like him, if I didn't know what he's been, and I say that even knowing what he *is*. Do you want to know the kind of a deal he came to me with? I'd help him get Bolan, he'd get the credit and see that I cashed in on the hundred grand bounty. Now that's what brought him to me in the first place."

"And your reaction?"

"Don't insult me, Braddock," Conn snorted. "You know how I feel about cops on the make. Twenty years ago I would have thrown him in a cell and clawed my way to an indictment. Just like you're wanting to do now. If there's one thing a man learns on this desert, though, it's patience. A month or a year makes damn little difference out here. I still haven't given Pena his answer. I've got him on the hook and I'm keeping him there. Meantime, he's on ice. Or he *was*, until you bulled in."

"What kind of hook?" Braddock asked, exhibiting remarkable self-control.

"We're bargaining. He knows I'm not too interested in the money. But he's got something else I'm willing to bargain for, and he knows it. Understand this, Braddock. Those boys busted my town, and I'm not standing for it. I want them, all of them, every damn one."

"What sort of bargaining?" the Captain persisted.

"It's been two weeks of Paris Peace Talks. I say something like, 'Well, let's see here now, Lou. I'll give you two of Bolan's fingers for three Mafia heads.' And he says, 'Well, you better let me think about that, Genghis.' He thinks about it for a day or so, then he comes back with a counteroffer. It's never enough, so I try to jack him up a little more."

"Are you levelling with me, Genghis?"

"Of course I'm levelling."

"What makes Pena so sure you have anything at all to offer him?"

Conn shrugged his shoulders. "I keep him pumped up. Look, Braddock, I told you the guy is scared to go home. Now the longer he stays away, the harder it gets to go back empty-handed. I told you I've got him hooked."

Braddock stared dreamily out the window. "It's a fool's game, Genghis," he said softly.

"Unless you've got some *real* bargaining power on your side."

"Okay, so I've got that," Conn replied, his eyes dropping.

"I guess you'd better tell me about it."

"I guess you'd better go to hell."

Braddock sighed. "For the next five minutes, we're off the record. After that ... well, I just hope you've got clean skirts, Genghis. If you've got *Bolan* on ice somewhere, too, then ..."

"That sounds like a threat, Captain."

"It is."

Conn bent to the floor and retrieved his hat. He put it on and rocked back in the swivel chair, added a fresh wad of tobacco leaves to the cud in his mouth, and chewed furiously for a minute. Then he sighed and said, "I believe Bolan got his face lifted here at Palm Village."

A muscle bunched in Braddock's jaw. He fixed Conn with a wide-eyed stare and said, "Where? By whom?"

"Up at the New Horizons."

"Is there a plastic surgeon there? Is that a ... well, Goddammit, Genghis! New Horizons! Are you telling me that's a plastics clinic?"

"Thought you knew," Conn said mildly, concentrating on his chew.

"Conn, I'm going to bust you for this!" Braddock spluttered.

"My five minutes ain't up yet," Conn replied, eyes twinkling.

"Five *minutes!*" Braddock yelled. "I could get you *five years!*"

"Yeah, but you already gave me five minutes," Conn pointed out. He scratched at the fresh scar traversing his ribs, tilted his hat further down across his forehead, and said, "And now I'm giving *you* five *seconds* to get your fat ass outta

126

my office. Beat it, Big City. Run and get your warrants."

Resisting suggestions that he "mob up" at the DiGeorge villa, Mack Bolan had maintained his accommodations at the resort hotel in Palm Springs while enjoying a free and ostensibly unrestricted run of the estate. He knew, of course, that few of his movements within the villa went unwatched and he suspected the existence of hidden observation posts behind various walls and ceilings. He had even discovered "bugs" in his hotel room. He had nevertheless managed to gather considerable intelligence concerning the combine's operations, such as the information he had been passing to Carl Lyons of the Pointer Detail. Contacts with Andrea D'Agosta had been both rare and fleeting, and characterized by a marked hostility on the girl's part. Through idle conversation with the other "soldiers," Bolan had learned that the girl had been but 20 years of age when her husband of less than a year drowned in a boating accident near San Pedro two years prior to Bolan's entry into Andrea's life. She was, of course, tolerated and deferred to by the palace guard but—as far as Bolan could determine—not actually liked by many of the men in DiGeorge's command. She was "the *Capo's* kid" and as such could do no wrong. She was variously referred to as "the American beauty rose"—"Miss Hotass"—"Th' damn debbatant"—and "Deej's bitter harvest"—none of these, however, within earshot of DiGeorge or his daughter or any of the officers in the guard.

Bolan had managed to identify himself with the common soldier. though most of them understood that he was "in probate" and undoubtedly destined for high rank in the organization. They

127

talked freely in his presence and delighted in the gossipy tidbits which Bolan dropped in their midst from time to time. In less than a week of in-and-out presence at the villa, Bolan already could boast a considerable cadre who were ready to follow him up the trail of exaltation. "Franky Lucky's going to get a territory," was the consensus, and many bored (and relatively poor) palace guards were hopeful of being taken into his crew when the big day arrived. Bolan encouraged this type of thinking, though never overtly, and was quietly marking certain soldiers for his possible use in an emergency.

As Bolan was departing the villa on the night of October 21st, he took the short cut across the patio to reach the parking area, resulting in one of his infrequent encounters with Andrea D'Agosta. She was seated beside the pool in a deck chair and wore a light wrap over her bathing costume. Bolan paused beside her chair and said quietly, "How's it been, Andrea?"

"Oh it's just been a ball," she replied in a dull voice. Her eyes flashed up to his then and her face became animated. "Haven't you been told that the pool is out of bounds to you hoods?"

"I guess I forgot," Bolan replied. He smiled. "No, that isn't true. I was hoping I might run into you."

"You 'ran into' me once too often, Mr. Lambretta," she said coldly.

"I'm sorry, Andrea," he told her, and moved on.

"You'll be a lot sorrier when Victor Poppy gets back from Florida!" the girl hissed.

It was more the tone of voice than her words that halted Bolan. He spun slowly on his heel and retraced his steps to stand in front of the deck chair. "What do you mean?" he asked in a subdued voice.

Andrea's eyes darted about the patio. She lifted her arms to him and pursed her lips. Bolan bent to the embrace but she avoided his kiss, moving her mouth to his ear. "They think you might be a phoney," she whispered. "I'm betting you are. What is it ... FBI or Treasury?"

Bolan pulled her out of the chair and clasped her to him, burying his lips into the soft flesh below her ear. "What's this about Florida?" he murmured.

"Phil Marasco sent a goon there to get a man out of jail. The man says he knew you, years ago, in New Jersey."

Bolan kissed her full on the mouth. She gasped and curled her fingers into his hair. "Get me out of here, Franky," she moaned.

"Don't worry, I will," he assured her. "Just play it cool. You understand?"

She nodded and began silently crying. "It's awful to feel this way about your own poppa, but I hate him," she sobbed. "I just *hate* him!"

"Save the hate for someone who deserves it," Bolan advised her.

"He deserves it, all right," she said. "I want you to look into something for me, Frank. Promise."

They kissed again. Bolan said, "What makes you so sure of *me*, Andrea?"

She ignored the parry. "Promise!" she hissed.

He nodded. "What do you want me to do?"

"Find out how Chuck *really* died," she whispered.

Bolan furrowed his brow and said, "Who's Chuck?"

"Charles D'Agosta, my husband."

Bolan stiffened and drew away to stare into

her eyes. She read the question in the gaze and nodded her head emphatically. Bolan grunted, "I heard he drowned."

"Chuck was an expert yachtsman," she whispered. "And he could swim before he could walk. Promise me you'll look into it."

Bolan said, "I promise. Now what about this Florida deal? Who's the guy?"

"I don't know. But they're bringing him here to confirm your identity."

"If you hear something else, let me know. Get word to me somehow."

"Then you really *are* someone else," she whispered excitedly.

Bolan grinned and stepped away from her. "Maybe I just don't like surprises," he said. He blew her a kiss and went on across the patio.

As he rounded the corner to the parking area, a figure moved out of the shadows and held up two fingers in the peace sign. Bolan recognized the smooth-faced youth who had been assigned to Andrea's guard.

"I spell peace p-i-e-c-e," the bodyguard said with a low chuckle.

"So do I," replied Franky Lucky Bolan. He squeezed the youth's shoulder and went on to his car.

The boy held the door for him as he climbed inside, then closed it and leaned down to peer admiringly through the open window. "When you leave here, Lucky, I'd be proud to go with you," he confided.

Bolan winked and said, "I'll remember that, Benny Peaceful."

The bodyguard grinned delightedly. "Hey, that's a name that could stick," he said.

"Bet on it," replied Bolan. He wheeled around, flashed his lights at the gate guards, and sped through with a clutch-jumping whine of the powerful engine.

"There goes Franky Lucky on the prowl again," observed one of the guards.

"I'm glad my name ain't Mack the Blacksuit Bolan," said the other.

"Ain't I," replied the first quietly, staring after the fast-disappearing tail lights.

Chapter Eighteen

THE INTERROGATION

Philip Marasco awakened Julian DiGeorge at shortly past dawn on the morning of October 22nd and said, "Five of the boys are missing, and I think they've gone out to join up with Pena."

"Who are they?" DiGeorge growled sleepily.

Marasco thrust a coffee-royal into his *Capo's* hands and inserted a lighted cigarette between his lips. "What's left of his old crew," the chief bodyguard reported. "Willie Walker and that bunch. I bet they've known where he was all this time."

"You better get the word to Franky Lucky," DiGeorge said.

"I already tried. Too late. He's gone. I'd guess he's up there right now for the hit. You want me to send 'im a crew?"

DiGeorge's eyes focused on the clock. He sipped at the laced coffee, took a drag on the cigarette, then looked again at the clock. "Naw," he said finally. "Too late for that now. I guess we get to see, Phil, just how good this Frank Lucky is, eh?"

"It's not even likely odds, Deej," Marasco worriedly pointed out.

DiGeorge sighed. "I wouldn't be so sure. Let's wait'n see before we start mourning our dead, eh? You better get a couple of cars ready, just in case though."

Marasco moved abruptly toward the door. He whirled about to say something, changed his mind, and went out the door muttering to himself, "I guess that's about all we can do now."

Lou Pena stirred, then sat bolt upright on the bed. A quiet voice announced, "It's okay, Lou, it's me, Willie."

The bedside lamp came on. Willie Walker, smiling grimly, leaned over the bed and fitted a key into the handcuffs with which Pena was manacled to the metal bedpost. "When did they start the bracelets routine?" he asked.

"Just last night," Pena whispered. "Christ, it's about time you was showing up. I had the signal out since yesterday afternoon." He drew his hand free and massaged the wrist, then reached hurriedly for his clothing. "This guy blew it, and the L.A. cops are after Lou Baby's ass."

"No need to be quiet," Walker informed him. "We got the cop."

Pena grunted. "How about the old lady?"

"Her, too. You better hurry it, though. This Franky Lucky might be making it here most any time."

Pena staggered into his trousers and said, "Who the hell is Franky Lucky?"

"Oh hell, there's a lot been going on you don't know about," Walker told him. "This Franky Lucky is a rodman from the East. He's got a contract on you, Lou."

Pena's eyes flipped wide with alarm. "Awww," he said unbelievingly. "Deej wouldn't go that far."

"The hell he wouldn't." Walker had knelt and was slipping socks on Pena's feet as the grizzled Mafia veteran was struggling into his shirt. "He thinks you made a singin' deal with the cops. The boys have been lighting candles all night. They're even making plans for a secret wake."

Pena's fingers fumbled with the buttonholes at the shirtfront. He seemed stunned. "We gotta get to 'im," he mumbled. "He's gotta call it off. I just

134

about got this thing sewed up now. You get on a phone, Willie, and tell 'im. I'm right in Bolan's tracks now. Tell Deej that Bolan got a face job, right here in th' Village. Tell 'im I been all this time finding that out. Tell Deej I also know the guy that give 'im the face job, and I'm right now finding out what this Bolan looks like now. You tell 'im that, Willie, and get 'im to call off this hit."

Walker nodded his head in somber agreement. "I'll try, Lou, but you know how these things go. Whattaya got in mind? I mean . . ."

"I'm going after this plastics man. You know the place, this rest home on the east side."

Walker appeared dazed. "Well hell, I guess we should'a known," he said. "Listen. Four boys are watching outside. Don't worry, they're with you. You take 'em on over there. I'll try to call Deej from here, then I'll join you over there later. But we better make it quick. Somebody comes in here and finds the cop and his old lady and some hell is gonna cut loose in this town."

Pena slipped into his coat. "You know how much I 'preciate this, Willie."

"Sure, sure," Walker said. He handed Pena a gun and dropped some loose bullets into his coat pocket. "You better beat it."

Bolan's Mercedes rolled quietly through the early-morning stir of the village, past the blackened hulk of Lodetown, and halted at an outside phone booth two blocks beyond the square. He consulted the directory, found Robert Conn's home address, then drove three blocks further on and parked the Mercedes on a side street several doors down from the Conn residence. He opened a gun case, withdrew a long-barreled .38, checked the load and spun the cylinder, affixed a silencer,

135

and jammed the weapon into the waistband of his trousers, then walked up the alley behind the row of houses.

He found Genghis and Dolly Conn in their bloodsoaked bed, their throats slashed, the bodies cold in death. Bolan muttered his regrets and quickly searched the rest of the house. Finding nothing of value, he immediately withdrew and returned to his vehicle. He put the car in motion and slowly circled the block once, pondering the unexpected development. Then a chilling thought struck him. He wheeled the Mercedes about and proceeded directly to New Horizons. He parked at the rear beside a dark Plymouth, noted a radio microphone clipped to the dashboard of that vehicle, and cautiously entered the clinic. He paused just inside the door and elevated his head, as though sniffing the air, then drew the .38, checked the snub .32 reposing in the sideleather, and advanced quietly to Jim Brantzen's private quarters.

Big Tim Braddock lay just inside the door to Brantzen's apartment, curled on his side, blood soaking into the carpet under him. A pistol lay several feet away. Bolan knelt quickly and felt Braddock's forehead. It was clammy. Bolan grunted and stepped cautiously into the kitchen.

He found Jim Brantzen, clad only in pajama bottoms, stretched out on the dining table, his head dangling over the edge. Bloodied pliers and wirecutters lay beside him on the table. Bolan winced and a guttural snarl tore up through the constrictions of his throat as he inspected his friend's mutilated body. Of all the atrocities Bolan had witnessed in the hamlets of Vietnam, he had never seen anything to equal the ferocity of this obvious interrogation. They had twisted the nipples out of his chest, probably with the pliers.

The entire torso was a raw pulp of mutilated meat. The ribs gleamed through bare spots where the flesh had been stripped away. The surgical fingers of the right hand had been whittled to the bone. Both earlobes were missing, his nostrils were slit up both sides, laying bare the bridge of his nose, and deep grooves had been carved beneath each eye. Worst of all, to Bolan's way of thinking, the hideously tortured surgeon was still alive ... and aware.

His breath was coming in ragged gurgles, blood bubbles forming about the mutilated nostrils, and all in the overtones of a ceaseless moaning. A bloodsmeared bottle of whiskey stood on a nearby stand, a stained towel lay in a pan of cold water; evidence, to Bolan, that the valiant surgeon had been repeatedly forced to maintain consciousness.

Bolan's hands moved carefully beneath his friend's head and he tenderly lifted it. "Who did it, Jim?" he asked with a shaking voice. "Who did this?"

Brantzen's eyes flared, dulled, then flared again. The lips moved, dribbling a red foam in the painful whisper: "They ... called him ... Lou."

Bolan nodded. "I know him. I'll get him, Jim."

"He ... knows ... sketch ... has sketch."

"I'm going to get him, Jim."

"He ... He ... knows ..." The right hand jerked up; glazed eyes stared at the skeletonized fingers; then the eyes closed, and Jim Brantzen died.

Tears squeezed past Bolan's tightening eyelids. He groaned, "Oh, *God!*" ... then he gently let Brantzen's head down and walked jerkily into the other room. Braddock's eyes were open and he had rolled onto his back. Bolan knelt over him, opened the coat, and found the wound. The big cop had caught it in the gut. "You okay?" Bolan asked him.

"No," Braddock wheezed.

"How long ago, Braddock?"

"Five minutes ... maybe ten."

"Hang on, I'll get an ambulance," Bolan told him. He went quickly out the door, through the lobby, and into Brantzen's surgical chamber. There he found compresses and hurried back with them to the fallen policeman. Bolan peeled away the clothing and applied the compresses to the wound.

"I'll bet you make it," he told Braddock.

The Captain merely stared at him, obviously in too much pain for conversation.

"I hope you do," Bolan added. He returned to the lobby, phoned for an ambulance, and made a hasty exit. Moments later, the powerful Mercedes was screaming around the curves of the high road to Palm Springs. Bolan thought he knew where he could intercept a torture-murderer. He was, in fact, betting his very life on it.

Chapter Nineteen

THE HIT

The six men were squeezed into the speeding car, Willie Walker in the front seat with a veteran triggerman named Bonelli and a younger wheelman who was called Tommy Edsel because of his one-time membership in a club of Edsel automobile enthusiasts. Screwy Lou Pena, all expansive smiles and high humor, took up nearly half of the rear seat. Wedged in with him were one Mario Capistrano, who had been recently released from the Federal Reformatory at Lompoc, and Harold the Greaser Schiaperelli, a 59-year-old Italian-born contract specialist who had been deported three times but had never spent a night behind bars.

Willie Walker freed an arm and leaned over the backrest, saying, "Lemme take a look at that picture, huh Lou?"

"Nothing doing," Pena objected, happily patting his jacket pocket. "Deej gets first look at this little jewel." He smiled archly and added, "After all, it's my passport back to the livin', Willie. Let's not be throwing it around the car, huh?"

"You're not forgetting," Walker pouted, "that us guys put our necks right up there with yours."

"I'm not forgetting," Pena assured him. "Don't you ever get to thinking that way, Willie. And Deej won't hold nothing against you when I explain this was all in the plan. He might be a little sore but he'll get over that quick enough. When he sees this picture, eh? Hell. Didn't he tell me not to come back without Bolan's head? Well, I got it." He tapped the pocket again. "I got Bolan's head."

"Hell it ain't even a picture," Tommy Edsel remarked. "It's just a drawin', ain't it?"

"Yeah but *what* a drawin'," Pena said. "A drawin' for a face job ain't just no *drawin'*, you know. Hell, it's a blueprint."

"That back there made me sick at my stomach," Capistrano complained. "I never saw a guy turned into a turkey like that before."

"Yeah but don't you forget, Mario, a *singing* turkey," Pena said. "Hell, I don't enjoy that kind of stuff any more than anyone else. His own damn fault, you gotta say that."

"You did that to his fingers *after*," Capistrano grumbled.

"That was for the lesson," Pena patiently explained. "Those guys gotta know they can't get away with it. Don't worry me with no blues now, Mario. Today's my day and I'm gonna enjoy it. You wanta walk back to the Springs, just say it."

"I wonder what about Franky Lucky," Bonelli fretted, perhaps only to change the subject.

"What is this Franky Lucky?" Pena snorted. "Some kinda goddam greaser golden boy?"

"Watch it," Willie Walker suggested in a low voice, his eyes shifting meaningfully to Harold the Greaser.

Pena laughed. "Aw hell, Willie, Harold ain't sensitive about being foreign born. Are you, Harold?"

Harold muttered something unintelligible and laughed. Pena laughed with him, although obviously he did not understand the comment. "Everybody's happy today," Pena observed.

"Except maybe Franky Lucky," Walker said. "Now Lou . . . this guy is as cold as a fish. And you were about right, he's a golden boy, at least

140

as far as Deej is concerned. And he's got his contract. And Deej says we'll just have to avoid him the best we can until he calls in or comes in. And the way Deej talked, this boy ain't going to be listening to anything we might have to say. He's going to shoot first and save the polite conversation for after."

"Didn't you say he's handling the hit personally?" Pena asked thoughtfully.

"This guy's a loner, Lou," Bonelli piped up. "They tell me he never takes no one along."

"Well hell, there's six of us, ain't there?" Pena said. "Anyway, he's not gonna be gunning for us between here'n home. Is he? What the hell are you worried about?"

The wheelman glanced over his shoulder and said, "Don't Franky Lucky wheel a blue sleek Mercedes?"

"Yeah, *some* kind of hot wheels," Walker replied. "Why?"

Tommy Edsel's head was now wagging to and fro as his eyes moved rapidly from his own route to a winding road descending from the hills to their right. "I bet that's him," he said ominously.

All eyes turned to the mountain road, about a quarter-mile distant. "You sure got better eyes than me, Tommy," Pena said, squinting with his forehead pressed against the window.

"Just keep looking," Tommy Edsel replied, his head still wagging rhythmically. "He's in and out. Look for a flash of blue. *There!* Did you see? Shit, man, that's him, that's Franky Lucky! And is he *wheeling!*"

As alarmed sounds rose up around him, Pena braked, "Awright awright, settle down. *If* it's him, and it probably ain't, just remember there's one of him and six of us. He ain't likely to try nothing. He'll trail along and wait for a chance.

141

He ain't gonna highway duel us, that's for damn sure."

"With Franky Lucky," Walker said worriedly, "nothing's for damn sure."

"Where do these roads come together?" Pena asked. He wet his lips nervously, affected by his companions' alarm.

"Just around this next curve," Tommy Edsel reported, "where the highway turns back toward the hills."

"Well dammit, you gotta beat him there!" Pena exclaimed.

"Dammit don't think I'm not trying," the wheelman replied, grunting with excitement. "But this boltpile sure as hell ain't no Mercedes!"

Pena and Walker were lowering their windows and the others were squirming about in the tight space trying to get their weapons ready.

"Just watch where you're shooting!" Pena yelled. "You guys onna other side be careful!"

Bolan had recognized the big Mafia vehicle at almost the same instant he had been spotted by Tommy Edsel. His visibility from the mountainside was unrestricted and gave him a panoramic sweep of the flatlands from the south horizon to the north. No other vehicles were in view; indeed, there was nothing but desolation for as far as the eye could see. He ran a quick mental triangulation on the speeding vehicles and smiled grimly at the incredibly perfect timing of his gamble. He would beat them to the junction by perhaps ten seconds; it would be ten seconds enough. The precision driving required to traverse the winding mountain road at such speeds had taken the full use of all his faculties, both mental and physical. There had been little left of Mack Bolan to mull over the unspeakable atrocity he had left behind at Palm Village ... and just as well. Beneath his peaking consciousness lurked a consuming rage such as this normally unemotional man had never experienced. His executions of the past had always been performed with a cool detachment, his combat-trained instincts dominating and guiding the actions of the mission. Never before had Bolan stepped forward with *rage* governing his performance, not even while avenging the deaths of his own father, mother, and sister. But that rage was there now, just below the surface. It was about to erupt ... and, with it, the full potency and ferocity of the Executioner.

Chapter Twenty

BETWEEN HORIZONS

The Mercedes slid to a halt at the intersection with screaming rubber. Bolan was outside and standing alongside almost before the forward motion was halted. He tossed his pistols to the shoulder of the road and quickly leaned back into the vehicle, depressing the clutch with one hand and shifting into low gear with the other. Then he ripped the rubber accelerator peddle away and forced the rod to full depression, wedging it into the hold of the floorboard. The big engine was screaming in full idle, reminding Bolan of a jet engine run-up. He dropped to his knees on the roadway, shifted his right hand over to the clutch pedal, and held the door with his left. He knew that he had to depend entirely upon visibility; he would not be able to hear the approach of the other vehicle through the whine of his own engine. His visibility extended for about three car-lengths beyond the intersection; both reflexes and timing would have to be perfect.

Then came the flash of motion at the edge of vision, and he was lunging clear of the Mercedes, allowing his own bodily motion to jerk his hand free of the clutch pedal. The powerful vehicle leapt forward like an arrow from a bow, the slamming door missing Bolan's shoulder by a hair, and Bolan completed his roll with both pistols in his fists.

"We've beat him!" Pena yelled triumphantly.

"We better had!" Tommy Edsel cried. "At a hunnert'n ten I ain't stoppin' nowhere soon!"

And then they were flashing into the intersection and catching first glimpse of the blue sports car nestled just outside the junction on the intersecting road. For a startled instant Pena wondered what the guy was doing on his knees beside the car; another microsecond and his finger was tightening on the trigger of his gun even as wheelman Tommy Edsel's reflexes began deciding to brake and turn.

The blue lightning bolt proved faster than Tommy Edsel's reflexes, however, and his foot was still heavy on the accelerator when the other car leapt into the intersection with a powering screech.

Willie Walker screamed, "Look out ... !" just as the Mercedes crunched against the right front fender in a grinding impact of protesting metal and showering glass. The velocity of the heavier car swung the Mercedes into a centrifugal tailspin, almost welding it to the side of the Mafia vehicle in another shattering impact. Willie Walker was thrown over Bonelli's head and rag-dolled into the windshield almost directly in front of Tommy Edsel. Harold the Greaser screamed something in Italian as Capistrano and Pena descended on him.

Expert wheelman Tommy Edsel fought the crazily spinning motion of the paired vehicles for another microsecond, and then the Mercedes was falling away, leaving the larger car to plunge on alone. The rear wheels moved out in front, jumped the shoulder, and then they were shuddering into soft sand and the big car was heeling over and going into its first roll.

Bolan had only a momentary glimpse of contorted faces and two protruding gun arms and then the two cars were together and moving away from him in a spinning plunge along the

146

main road. He ran along in pursuit but was far behind even before the Mercedes dropped away and spun off into the scrubby desert. It seemed to be happening in slow motion, with the big vehicle coming around in a gentle swing and leaving the highway several hundred feet beyond. Its rear wheels slid gracefully onto the sand, dug in, and the heavy car began rolling sideways in a wide arc back toward the intersection, disgorging curiously flopping bodies along the way. Bolan counted six rolls before the journey ended in a wheels-up settling of mangled metal.

Tommy Edsel was still clutching the collapsed steering wheel when Bolan reached the wreckage. Blood was oozing from both corners of his mouth as he hung there in the seat belt. The entire front seat had moved forward; Tommy's chest had apparently been crushed by the steering wheel, but he turned his head and gave Bolan a glazed, upside down stare. Bolan shot him once between the eyes and moved around to the other side of the inverted automobile.

Bonelli was twisted into a caved-in section of the roof, partially pulped and obviously dead. Bolan wrestled his head clear, just the same, and shot him between the eyes. Then he began the back track of strewn bodies.

Willie Walker was the nearest. Part of his head was missing and the legs were bent into an impossible configuration under his back; Bolan had to settle for a bullet between where the eyes had been.

Harold the Greaser Schiaperelli was next. He was partially decapitated and one hand was missing. Bolan drilled another hole between the gaping eyes.

Mario Capistrano lay on his side in the sand. He was weeping and contemplating a number of jagged ribs which protruded from his side. Bolan rolled him face up, said, "Close your eyes," and promptly gave him a third one which could not be closed.

Lou Pena was on his knees, watching Bolan's advance. His right arm was missing, from the elbow down. The nose was smashed and two teeth protruded through his lower lip. In a strangely quacking Donald Duck voice, he said, "I got it. I got Bolan's head."

"Do tell," Bolan said, and shot him between the eyes. He caught the torn body as it toppled forward and felt through the pockets, finding Brantzen's sketch next to Pena's heart.

Bolan struck a match and held the flame under the sketch, turning it carefully to insure an even burn. Then he scattered the ashes in a fine powder across the sands as he retraced his steps to the roadway. He returned to the Mercedes, looked it over, and wrote it off. He opened the gas tank and encouraged a flow across the parched land until he was a safe distance removed, then he struck another match and touched it to the spillage.

The flames raced quickly along the gasoline trail. Bolan was already trudging toward the Palm Springs and did not even look back when the explosion came. A terrible force was afoot in the land, he was thinking, when a man like Jim Brantzen could be reduced to a mound of mutilated meat by the likes of that back there.

And there were more, like those back there, *up* there across that horizon. Mack Bolan's *new horizon* had never been closer, nor more passionately sought. Death on the hoof was moving toward Palm Springs.

Chapter Twenty-One

THE SQUEEZE

The sun was approaching the high point in the sky when Bolan staggered into Palm Springs, picked up a taxi, and went on to his hotel. The desk clerk gaped at this appearance and said, "Did you have an accident, Mr. Lambretta?"

"I lost my car," Bolan told him. "Get me another one just like it, will you."

The clerk's chin dropped another inch. "Yes *sir*," he replied crisply.

"Send up a couple of buckets of ice."

"Yes sir, and the liquids that go with it?"

"Just the ice," Bolan said tiredly. "I'll need the car in an hour." He swung about and wobbled toward the elevator.

"Uh, Mr. Lambretta, we might have to compromise a bit on the color. The Mercedes, I mean."

"I said *just like it*," Bolan snapped back. He went on up to his room, stripped off the sweat-soaked clothing, and moved immediately to the bath. Shocked by his own dust-streaked image in the mirror, he scowled at the still strange mask of Frank Lambretta, stepped into the shower, and luxuriated there for several minutes, frequently raising his face into the spray to suck the water into the parched membranes of his mouth and throat.

Two small plastic containers of crushed ice were on the dressing table when he returned to the bedroom. The dust- and sweat-encased clothing had been removed; his revolvers lay on the bed beside a layout of fresh underwear.

149

Bolan got into the underwear and stuffed a small snowball into his mouth, then reached for the telephone and called the unlisted number in DiGeorge's study. Phil Marasco's voice broke into the first ring. "Yes?" he said softly.

"This is Frank," Bolan said. "Tell Deej that order's been filled."

A short pause, then: "Okay, Franky, I'll tell him. Where are you?"

"At the hotel. I'm beat. I'll be in pretty soon."

Bolan could hear DiGeorge's quiet rumble in the background but could not distinguish the words. Marasco said, "Deej wants to know about the picture."

"What picture?"

"The subject was supposedly carrying a surgeon's sketch of another interesting subject. Do you have it?"

"Of course not," Bolan sorted. "I don't go around collecting souvenirs."

Another background rumble, then: "He wants to know where you left that contract."

"Where the mountain meets the desert," Bolan reported cryptically, "and where one subject might wait for another."

"Okay, I got that. Deej says come home as soon as possible."

"Tell Deej I took a five-mile stroll in the sun. Tell him I'll be home when I can forget that."

Marasco chuckled. "Okay, Franky, I'll tell him. Get yourself rested, then come on out. There's things you should know about."

"I'll be there," Bolan said. He hung up, stared at the floor for a moment, then opened a fresh pack of cigarettes, lit one, and stretched out across the bed.

"Yes, I'll be there," he repeated in a dull monotone, speaking to himself. "With bells."

Philip Marasco led the search party out the little-travelled desert blacktop which links Palm Springs and Palm Village. Two cars, each carrying five men, made the short trip to the crossroads and found the scene of Franky Lucky's "hit" with no difficulty whatever.

The ten *Mafiosi* ran excitedly about the scene of action, poking, pointing, and animatedly reconstructing the details. Marasco searched each body thoroughly, went over the vehicle with precision, then arranged his troops at arm's-length intervals for a wide scrutiny along the entire length of the death car's travel.

Returning to the villa, Marasco dolefully reported to his *Capo*, "If Lou had a sketch, he must've ate it. And you should see the mess this Franky Lucky made of those boys. I never saw nothing like it."

"It don't make sense that he had no sketch," DiGeorge argued fretfully. "He had to have *something* up his sleeve or he wouldn't have been beating it back here. I guess there was nothing left alive, eh?"

"Not hardly," Marasco replied, shuddering. "There wasn't hardly anything left even *whole*. I never saw such a mess. This Franky Lucky is a mean contractor. And let me tell you, Deej, he don't mess around on a hit. Remember those six-to-one odds we was talking about last night?"

DiGeorge soberly nodded his head. "Didn't mean much, eh?"

"It wouldn't have meant anything at *twelve* to one, Deej. I tell you, when this Franky Lucky *does* find himself a piece of that Bolan, I want to be around to see what happens."

DiGeorge was staring thoughtfully into empty space. He noisily cleared his throat and said, "I wonder if you've thought of something, Phil. I wonder if you realize that someone has been playing games with old Deej."

Marasco inspected his *Capo's* face, found no clue to his thoughts, and replied, "What kind of games, Deej?"

"What was it Franky Lucky was telling me about this fight he had with Bolan? He said he saw Bolan down at the corners, and he recognized him, and they shot it out. And this was just a few days after Bolan ducked us over at th' Village. Right?"

"Yeah." Marasco was chewing the thought. "But I ..." His eyes widened and he said, "Whuup! Willie Walker says on the phone that Bolan got his face carved the day of the hit."

"That's just what I been thinking, Philip Honey," DiGeorge mused. "Now somebody has got a story crossed. I wonder who?"

"Why would Franky want to cross you up, Deej?"

"That's what I have to wonder about, Phil. We're just saying *if*, now. *If* Screwy Looey was telling it straight. Have you ever caught Lou in a lie, Phil? I mean *ever*? An *important* lie?"

Marasco was thinking about it. He shook his head and replied, "I don't believe Lou ever gave you anything but a straight lip, Deej. But we got to remember one thing. Lou could have *thought* he had something. Maybe someone else wanted him to think that."

"You ever know any boys that got face jobs, Phil?"

"Yeah. It used to be the fashion back East."

"How long before they're out of bandages?"

"Oh, two or three weeks."

DiGeorge grunted. "And the boys I knew, they went around with puss pockets and Band-Aids

152

for sometimes a month after that. It's a messy thing, this face job."

"They're even moving hearts around from body to body now, Deej. Maybe they got better ways to give face jobs now, too."

"I want somebody to find out about that," DiGeorge commanded.

"Sure, Deej."

"Meanwhile, Franky Lucky is right back in *probate*. If Bolan *did* get a face job, Franky didn't see him at no desert corners a few days later, no matter how fancy they get with face jobs. There's only one of two ways, saying that Bolan did get carved. He either saw him in bandages, or he saw him wearing the new face. Now that's plain, ain't it? *Franky Lucky could not have recognized Bolan three days after a face job!*"

"That's a fact, Deej," Marasco said. He appeared to be slightly out of breath. "Saying, of course, that Lou had the straight lip, then Franky Lucky has been using a curved one."

DiGeorge sighed. "That's a fact, Philip Honey." He sighed again. "You say the boy shoots a hard hit, eh?"

"You'd have to see what I saw, Deej, before you could ever know."

"Wouldn't it be hell," DiGeorge said tiredly, "if Franky Lucky turns out to be this Bolan's new face."

Marasco lost his breath entirely. His face paled. "I wouldn't go that far, Deej," he puffed.

"I would," DiGeorge stated matter-of-factly. "That's why I'm the *Capo*, Philip Honey. I would. When is Victor Poppy due in?"

"L.A. International at two o'clock," Marasco replied mechanically. "Franky might have lied a

153

little, Deej. About shooting it up with Bolan. Just to get your attention."

"I thought of that, too. I have to think of everything, Phil. Don't worry, I'm thinking. I sure want to see this gift Victor's bringing us."

"I'd have to guess that Franky Lucky is straight, Deej," Marasco stated, phrasing the strongest argument he dared.

"You do the guessing, Phil," DiGeorge replied with a weary smile. "I'll do the thinking."

Bolan stopped at a secluded public telephone booth and gambled on finding Carl Lyons at the contact number. The gamble paid off. Lyons immediately asked, "What do you know about the events at Palm Village early this morning?"

"Enough," Bolan said. "I'll trade some intel with you."

"No trades," Lyons clipped back. "Tim Braddock's at the point of death, and the most grisly damn piece of . . ."

"I know all about it, Lyons," Bolan said humbly. "Will Braddock make it?"

"The doctors are hopeful. At the very best, though, he'll be out of things for quite a while."

"He's a good cop," Bolan said, genuinely regretful.

"Better than some I know," Lyons replied in a faint self-mockery. "What'd you call about, Pointer?"

"My cover's in danger. I need some intel."

"Just a minute . . . Brognola's here and frothing. He was doubling up between us and Braddock, and . . . just a minute, Pointer."

Bolan heard a whispered consultation, then the light click of another receiver coming on the line.

"Okay," Lyons said. "Brognola's on with us.

154

You give us some words first. Who made that hit up there this morning, besides Pena?"

"I don't know all the names, but you can identify the remains," Bolan replied. "You'll find them scattered around the junction of the Palm Springs high and low roads. Six of them, including Pena."

"All dead," Brognola's smooth voice stated.

"That's right," Bolan said. "Now can we talk about my problem?"

"Who killed them?" from Brognola.

"Call it a double contract," Bolan said. "Julian DiGeorge got the idea that Pena has been informing. The other five boys were siding with Pena."

"Then the rubout had no connection with the murders of the Conns and the plastic surgeon?" Brognola asked.

"I didn't say that," Bolan replied.

Lyons snarled. "This guy is playing games with you, Hal. Bolan, you executed those men, didn't you!"

"Who's he talking to?" Bolan asked Brognola.

"They found out that Brantzen had altered your face, and they went up there to wring something out of him! That much is obvious so save all of us the time and stop playing games. You happened along, saw what they'd done to your doctor friend, and went gunning for them. Now you're saying that your cover is in jeopardy. What kind of information did Pena get back to the mob before you killed him, Bolan?"

"Just a moment, before you answer that, Mr. Pointer," Brognola said. "Please don't leave the line."

Again the sounds of a muted, off-phone discussion came to Bolan's ears. Then Brognola came back on. "Mr. Pointer," he said, "we appreciate

155

the work you've been doing for us, and we have no wish to compromise your position. You don't have to say anything to incriminate yourself."

"Fair enough," Bolan replied.

"We are not questioning your identity. Just tell us this much. Were the murders at Palm Village this morning ordered by Julian DiGeorge?"

"No," Bolan said. "It was all Pena's idea."

"I see. And now Pena and his squad are dead."

"That's right."

• "At DiGeorge's orders?"

"There was a contract out on Pena."

"I see," Brognola replied with some confusion.

Bolan sighed. "Okay, Lyons," he said. "I don't want you people to start questioning my intel. You're right, it's no time for games. Besides, I'm about as incriminated as one person can get already. This is Bolan. I've penetrated the DiGeorge family, and I pulled off the hit on Pena this morning. I was acting purely for myself on that one, though. You saw, or heard, what they did to Brantzen."

"Yeah," Lyons said softly. "Braddock gave a pretty good description of the guy who helped him, Bolan. It fits a man who was sitting in my car the other night, in Redlands."

"Yeah," Bolan said. "About my problem."

"Go ahead," Lyons sighed.

"I hear that the *Commissione* employs a private staff of enforcers. I need to know who runs that show."

"That's your department, Hal," Lyons said.

"Presently only ten bosses sit on the *Commissione*," Brognola reported. He rattled off the names. "You'll note that DiGeorge's name is not present. He walked out in a huff two years ago over some dispute about the narcotics traffic. He sits in from time to time, though, when some subject important to him comes up for discussion. Technically, he still has a voice on that council."

"But there are tensions?" Bolan asked interestedly.

"There are tensions," Brognola assured him. "The council wanted to regulate prices. DiGeorge won't go for it. He controls a big slice of their narcotic imports. He feels that the pricing is his affair, and he wholesales to the other families on his own terms. Yes, there are tensions."

"Thanks," Bolan said. "That gives me something to parlay. I'm especially interested in the council's enforcers, though. What can you tell me about that?"

Brognola coughed and said, "The Talifero brothers, it is said, have the most feared crew of enforcers in the country. These brothers are loosely called 'Pat and Mike.' They are . . ."

"Okay, I've heard of Pat and Mike. What you say wraps it up. Maybe I can keep my neck out of . . ."

"Be careful, Pointer," Brognola urged. "These Talifero boys are double trouble. It's said that once they get their orders, they are like guided missiles, there's no way of calling them back or scrubbing the hit. The triggermen in their crew are like an elite Gestapo, taking orders from no one but Pat and Mike. The brothers themselves operate directly out of the *Commissione*."

"Exactly what I wanted," Bolan commented. "I'd better bug off now."

"Uh, Pointer . . ." Brognola said hurriedly.

"Yes?"

"I'm flying to Washington tonight. I'd like to make a representation on your behalf."

"What sort of representation?"

"A sort of unofficial 'forgive and forget' representation. Do you follow me?"

"Who's playing games now?" Bolan said, chuckling.

"He's dead serious, Bolan," Lyons broke in.

Brognola said, "Rather, uh, high offices have been apprised of your successes here. We've suspected your true identity and now that you've confirmed it ... well ... I'm not promising anything, but ... I believe I can get you a portfolio—unofficially, you understand—if you'll agree to continue on in your present role."

"It is my intention to continue," Bolan said. "Unless I die soon."

"You aren't going to die soon, are you?" Lyons said, chuckling.

"Not if I can help it."

"Can we do anything to help?"

"I doubt it. I guess it's my show—win, lose, or draw. Uh, you might look into the death of one Charles D'Agosta two years ago, age about 20, supposedly drowned on a boating accident off San Pedro."

"Mafia rubout, Bolan?" Lyons asked.

"Let's call him Pointer," Brognola broke in nervously.

Bolan laughed and said, "The rubout is an outside chance. Look into it, will you?"

"I'll do that," Lyons assured him. "Anything else?"

"You might pray."

Lyons and Brognola chuckled. Bolan said, "Well ..."

"Braddock says thanks," Lyons added hastily.

Bolan said, "Sure," and broke the connection. He returned to the new Mercedes, checked his gunleather, and set off for the villa. Police-community relations had never seemed better for Mack Bolan. He wondered vaguely what was implied by acquiring a "portfolio."

"Maybe it's a license to kill," he muttered to his Mercedes. "And then again," he added thoughtfully, "maybe it's a license to die."

Either way, Mack Bolan was not too impressed with licenses. He had his rage to keep him warm.

Chapter Twenty-Two

THE ENFORCER

The gate guard grinned warmly and said, "Hi-ya, Franky. God, I heard about the fracture this morning. They say it was like a wild man. I wished I'd been with you."

Bolan kept his face straight and said, "You might get a chance, Andrew Hardy." He soberly winked one eye and eased on over to his usual parking place. He noted that the gate guard had trotted down to engage another guard in an animated conversation.

Benny Peaceful appeared as Bolan was leaving the Mercedes. He showed Bolan the peace sign and said, "Somebody has been waiting for you by the pool for a couple of hours. Somebody's gonna be terrible disappointed if you don't go in that way."

Bolan acknowledged the message with a nod of his head. He paused to light a cigarette and said, "What's rumbling, Benny?"

"The whole joint's rocking over your work this morning," the youth replied, laboring to maintain a sober visage. "Don't surprise me none, of course. I knew what you could do, Franky."

"I need your help, Benny Peaceful," Bolan said, staring over the boy's head. "I think I know what you can do, too."

Benny seemed to grow an immediate inch. Following Bolan's lead, he averted his eyes in a casual inspection of the sky. "You just say it, Franky Lucky," he said solemnly.

"A boy like you can change his thinking when the right time comes," Bolan suggested.

161

"You watch me."

"Pat and Mike could use a boy like that."

The youth's breath hurriedly left him. He staggered slightly, regained his balance, and then gave way to the glowing smile that was fighting for control of his facial muscles. "God!" he exclaimed. "I knew you was something special."

"A boy that knows when to keep quiet, and then when to come running at the right time—he can be a valuable boy," Bolan pointed out.

"You just snap your fingers, Franky Lucky," Benny assured him.

"Okay. You be ready for the snap." Bolan tossed away the cigarette and entered the enclosed patio. Benny Peaceful came in several paces to the rear and took up station against the wall, his face glowing like the sunrise. Bolan went back to him and said, "Listen, I made a decision. You're my second here. You know?"

The news was almost too much for Benny Peaceful. His lips trembled, he drew in a ragged breath, and he gasped. "I'm your boy, Franky. What's going on?"

Bolan leaned closer. "I told you, Benny, a valuable boy has to change his thinking. Deej is out. Understand?"

The youth nodded his head in an uncoordinated jerk. "I been hearing," he replied. "I been changing my thinking, since a long time back."

"Okay, now you round up the other boys that've been thinking. We don't want the good to go down with the bad, do we, Benny Peaceful? I'm making that your Number One job for right now. You mark the ones that are fit to save. You know?"

"God, I know, Franky."

"Okay. You get these boys aside. Boys who have been thinking ought to know that what hap-

162

pened on the desert this morning was nothing but a prophecy of things to come. You know what I'm saying?"

"Screwy Looey had that coming," Benny Peaceful agreed eagerly. "A lot of muscle around here has got it still coming."

"It'll get to 'em, don't you worry," Bolan declared somberly. "It's up to you, Benny, to cull out the others so they don't get hurt. I don't have the time, so I'm depending on you. Now you get these boys aside and you tell 'em what's what. And you tell 'em to wait for your fingers to snap."

Benny Peaceful fought down another broad grin. "*My* fingers? Sure—sure, Franky."

"Get your crew organized."

"I'll get right to work, Franky."

The youth took off on a strangely hurried-casual gait, disappearing around the corner to the parking area. Bolan clucked his tongue and went on over to the pool and Andrea D'Agosta.

"What was all the chatter with Boy Blue?" she asked him.

"Got rid of him, didn't I?" Bolan replied, smiling.

"Don't look so happy," she said. "I've been waiting out here for hours. I'm afraid your moment has almost arrived, whoever you are."

Bolan leaned down and brushed her cheek with his lips. "Yeah?"

"No time for that," Andrea fretted. "Victor Poppy is here with that man from Florida. They're all in Poppa's study right now."

Bolan clung to his smile. "Did you get this man's name?"

"I heard Victor call him Tony. That's all I know. Little man, sallow, skinny, scared. About 40."

163

Bolan sighed and said, "Thanks."

"Don't thank me, just get me out of here."

"Are you ready to go right now?" Bolan asked her.

Her eyes flipped wide. "Are you serious?"

"I guess it's now or never," he told her. He looked her over and added, "You're dressed fit to travel. Leave everything else behind. Do you know where you're going?"

"A bee-line to Italy," she said. "I'll visit Momma for a while."

"And you don't care what becomes of your father?"

Andrea stared curiously at Bolan for a moment, then: "Poppa didn't consult me when he went into this business."

Bolan took it as a reply. He said, "Okay, come on, I'll get you out of here. Then I have to . . ."

He had Andrea by the arm and was helping her out of the chair. Phil Marasco appeared in a doorway across the court and yelled at him. Bolan looked up and waved a greeting. "Deej is waiting for you," Marasco called out. "Come on, he's getting impatient."

Bolan released the girl. "Sit tight," he told her. "I'll be back."

"I wonder," she murmured, and fell back into the chair with an unhappy sigh.

Bolan walked briskly across the patio and joined Marasco in the doorway. "What's up?" he asked.

"I dunno," Marasco replied nervously. "Th' old man is sitting on needles, though, and he wants to see you in the worst way."

They walked elbow-to-elbow along the corridor toward DiGeorge's study. "I told him the order was filled," Bolan growled. "What's he worrying about?"

164

"He would have cancelled that hit if we could of got to you, Franky," Marasco confided. "Don't mention it, though, it'll just make him nervouser."

"You don't cancel hits, Philip Honey," Bolan snapped.

Marasco grunted and said, "Now you're talking like a family man."

"I like you, Phil," Bolan said, slowing his pace. Marasco slowed to match him.

"That's great, I like you too," he said without embarrassment.

"You know, in the old days of Egypt and places, when a king died they buried all his household with him. Servants, slaves, and everything."

"Yeah?"

"Sure. Those Egyptians figured when the king stopped living, all his cadre had a right to stop living too. Stupid, huh?"

Marasco halted completely. "What're you getting at, Franky?"

Bolan swung about to face him squarely. "Pat and Mike say a king has got to go, Philip Honey," he said soberly.

The blood drained from Marasco's face. He said, "Oh my God. I knew it was something like that."

"I been hoping you ain't no Egyptian, Philip Honey," Bolan said.

Marasco snatched a cigarette from his pocket and thoughtfully placed it between his lips. Bolan lit it. He took a deep drag and puffed the smoke out in tight grunts. Presently he said, "I'm not no Egyptian, Franky Lucky."

"I'm glad to hear that." Bolan began moving slowly toward DiGeorge's door. Marasco reached out and placed a restraining hand on his arm.

165

"Wait a minute," Marasco said. "Before you go in there. They got a turkey in there waiting for you."

"What kind of turkey?" Bolan asked casually.

"A guy says he knew you back when. But he says also you died in Vietnam, in the army. Is this guy part of your cover, Franky?"

"Maybe. What's his name?"

"Tony Avina. He says you grew up on his block in Jersey City. Says you got drafted and got killed. Is this gonna embarrass you in front of Deej?"

"Is this guy in the organization?" Bolan asked.

"Naw. A nobody. Prison gray sunk in all over him."

"Look, Phil," Bolan said conspiratorially, "my name ain't Frank Lambretta."

"Yeah, I figured that about a minute ago," Marasco replied. "So what're you gonna do about this turkey?"

"I'm gonna scare the turkey-shit outta him, that's what," growled Franky Lucky Bolan. "Come on. Let's go see what color he drops."

Carl Lyons paced the floor excitedly, glaring at Howard Brognola. "But this could be dynamite, Hal, if we could just get it into Bolan's hands!" he cried. "Somebody bought himself a coroner on this deal, and you know it as well as I. That inquest should have come out with murder written all over it."

"I know, I know," Brognola said gently. "But you have to remember, Carl, the name Lou Pena wasn't half the flag two years ago that it is now. There was never any suggestion that this Louis Pena who was driving the motorboat was the same infamous Lou Pena of the roaring thirties, no suggestion at all. The coroner could have quite

166

logically arrived at a valid decision when he ruled in favor of accidental death. The damages were settled out of court, no trial, no charges, no nothing, and everybody appeared satisfied all around."

"But for God's sakes," Lyons argued, "a sailing boat always has the right of way over a powered launch. The D.A. should have brought charges, if nobody else. Pena simply sliced through that little sailboat, hung around long enough to make sure the job was thorough, pleaded an unfortunate accident, and walked away with everybody happy. Now that's not justice, no matter how you slice it. We can even prove motive. You take a . . ."

"In aftersight," Brognola said, trying to calm the angry policeman. "There was no access to these records two years ago. Not even now, for ordinary circumstances. If I hadn't had a bell ring over that name D'Agosta, you still wouldn't have any lead on the motive."

"Well, I have to get hold of Bolan," Lyons said. "I have a boney feeling about this. Bolan is out there in a den of vipers, and he needs all the ammo we can feed him. Do you realize that we've *never* been able to get an informer *inside* the Mafia?"

"Do *I* realize?" Brognola replied, laughing.

"So okay," Lyons snapped. "Let's not mince around, with our man's neck on the block. Bolan gave us the number. I say we use it."

Brognola put on a pained expression. "That will have to be your decision," he said. "Call him there if you think you must. But don't ask me to second the motion."

Lyons unfolded a scrap of paper and stared at a telephone number written there. It had been included in the last package of information which had been passed to them by the man they had then known as Pointer.

The words "For Red Alert Only" were above the number, then the name "Lambretta," followed by a Palm Springs telephone number.

"I wonder where this telephone is located," Lyons muttered.

"I guess you'll never know until you call it," Brognola said.

"I could give it to the phone company. They'd run it down for me."

"By that time, perhaps the time for action will have passed," Brognola sighed.

"Yeah," Lyons said. He stared hesitantly at the telephone. Then he pulled the instrument toward him, acquired an outside line, began dialing, then abruptly re-cradled the transmitter. "Dammit," he muttered under his breath. "I wasn't cut out for this cloak-and-dagger stuff."

Bolan and Marasco strolled into the *Capo's* inner sanctum in controlled good humor. Marasco remained near the door. Bolan proceeded on, flipped a high-sign to DiGeorge, and dropped into a leather chair.

"A rest is a rest, Franky," DiGeorge groused, "but I didn't tell you to take all day."

Two other men were present. One of them was familiar to Bolan; he assumed that this was Victor Poppy. He recognized the other from Andrea's crisp description. Bolan looked the man over thoroughly during a hushed silence, playing the moment for its most, then said, "Hi-ya, Tony. When did you decide to retire from institutional life?"

DiGeorge began breathing again. Victor Poppy smiled nervously and flicked a glance at his boss. The little man in the hot seat was staring at Bolan with a frightened gaze. "Hi, Fr ..." His voice cracked. He choked, coughed, cleared his throat, and dabbed at eyes suddenly brimming with tears. He pounded weakly on his chest, smiled self-consciously, and settled back into the chair.

"You boys know each other?" DiGeorge asked in feigned surprise.

"People change a lot," Bolan said quietly. "Tony there used to be a real terror. Had half the guys in the neighborhood scared to death of him. Yeah ... people change."

"I guess *you* ain't changed a lot, Franky," Marasco said. "You're still lookin' like a young frisky colt."

Bolan did not miss the reproachful glance tossed at Marasco by Julian DiGeorge. He grinned. "Naw ... I'm changing, too," he said. "Take the present situation, now. Look at me, all tired and beat. Over a simple little everyday hit. Five years ago I could've rubbed six boys like that and stopped off for a few pieces o' tail on the way home. Now all I'm doing is *dragging* my tail."

Marasco laughed loudly. DiGeorge turned to him with a frown and Marasco promptly shut it off.

Victor Poppy said, "I heard about that, Franky. Everybody in the place is talking it up. I'd like to go out there and see that."

"Shuddup!" DiGeorge growled.

The effect of Bolan's braggadocio was already evident on the face of DiGeorge's "gift turkey," however. The small man was staring at Bolan with haunted eyes, nervously twisting his hands together. "It's good to see ya again, Frank," he chirped.

"Waitaminnit waitaminnit," DiGeorge yelled. He pointed an accusing finger at Tony Avina. "You was telling me not ten minutes ago that this

169

Frank Lambretta went off to war and got hisself killed! Now what, huh?"

"Jeez, I dunno, Mr. DiGeorge," Avina quavered.

"Lay off 'im, huh Deej?" Bolan said softly. "Can't you see he's sick?"

"Where do you get off telling me to lay off?" DiGeorge shouted. "Just who the hell do you think you are, Mr. Franky Lucky Phoney!"

"Who do *you* think I am, Deej?" Bolan asked quietly.

DiGeorge stared at him in speechless rage. Every movement, every word, every gesture of Franky Lucky since he entered that door had served to increase DiGeorge's irritability. Now this! Talking back, acting like a *Capo*, just like that first damn day with Andrea, just like ... A cold knot began to form in DiGeorge's belly, clamping off the line of thought. The rage dissolved instantly. "Okay," he said, now in perfect control, "you asked the question, Big Shot. Now you answer it."

Bolan's gaze shifted to Tony Avina. "Answer it, Tony," he said. "Tell Mr. Julian DiGeorge who I am. Tell him the damn truth."

"Jeez, I don't know who you are, Franky," Avina shot back.

Bolan became convulsed with laughter. Phil Marasco joined in, and then Victor Poppy. DiGeorge's chin trembled, then he began laughing also. Bolan got up and pounded on the wall with one hand, clutching at his stomach with the other, in a very convincing demonstration of rampant humor.

"Jeez, I don't know who I am either!" Bolan yelled and fell back into the chair gasping for breath and holding himself with both hands.

"Get this goddam turkey outta here!" Di-

George roared between snorting guffaws. "First thing comes up, I won't even know who I am!"

"Just a minute," Marasco said, sobering suddenly. "I guess I have to tell you, Deej. After all these years together, I got to tell you."

"Tell me what?" DiGeorge asked.

"Okay, Franky?" Marasco asked of Bolan.

Bolan, still chuckling, gave him the nod.

"About Franky Lucky. He's in the family."

"What family?" DiGeorge said, sobering and craning about to glare at Marasco.

"Vittorini," Bolan said quietly.

All chuckling and sniggering ceased as total quiet descended. DiGeorge slowly turned about to inspect "his boy" Franky Lucky whom he wanted to sponsor into his family and turn over the reins to some day. "I don't get you," he said thickly.

"I belong to the Vittorini Family," Bolan explained.

"He belongs to Pat and Mike," Marasco explained further.

DiGeorge opened his mouth and then snapped it shut. He looked from Bolan to Marasco and back to Bolan again. "What is this?" he asked quietly. "Tell me what this is, Philip Honey."

"You know what this is, Deej," Bolan said.

"No I guess I don't." DiGeorge had heaved to his feet and was walking warily toward his desk.

"You know what I want, Phil," Bolan stated softly.

Marasco beat DiGeorge to the desk and leaned against it. His hand went inside his jacket and stayed there.

"Hey what the hell is this?" DiGeorge asked, his voice shaking.

"You want me to take Deej out for some air, Franky?" Marasco said.

"He looks like he needs some," Bolan replied.

171

He relaxed further into his chair. "Yeah. He needs some air, Phil."

"You can't pull this shit!" DiGeorge yelled.

"I'm not pulling nothing, Deej," Bolan said. He smiled at Victor Poppy. "Hey, Victor, take your friend and go on back to Florida. Stay awhile. Get some sun. Tony looks like he could use some. And you ..."

"Where d'you get off telling my boys when to go and where to go?" DiGeorge screamed.

"Is that guy still here?" Bolan asked, still looking at Victor Poppy. "I thought Phil was taking him out for an airing. Huh? Is he still here?"

Victor Poppy was moving for the door, pushing Avina ahead of him. "What guy?" Victor Poppy asked nervously. "I don't see nobody but you and me and Tony, Franky."

"That's what I thought," Bolan said contentedly.

"You can't pull this shit!" DiGeorge screamed.

"The hell I can't," said Franky Lucky Bolan.

Chapter Twenty-Three

BLOOD SPRINGS

Victor Poppy and Tony Avina almost ran over someone in the corridor. Bolan could hear them apologizing. The .32 was in his hand and muzzling for the door when Andrea D'Agosta stepped through. In her hand was the little nickel-plated .22 Bolan had taken from her some days earlier.

She sized up the situation in a quick circular glance, then stared soberly at Bolan's weapon. Her nose quivering, she said, "I want my Poppa."

"Someone else already has him," Bolan told her.

"I take everything back," she said. "I want him."

"Andrea, get outta here," DiGeorge growled.

"I've been listening," she said. "I know what's going on here." Her eyes flared pure hatred at Mack Bolan. "You're worse than any of them," she spat. "I didn't want to believe the stories I've been hearing today but they're true. You're a kill-crazy hood and now you think you're going to kill my Poppa."

"Aw hey, *bambina*," DiGeorge pleaded. "Go on outta here and let us men handle our business. You got it all wrong."

"She has it all *right*, Deej," Bolan said.

"Well, for God's sakes ain't you got no sense of . . ."

DiGeorge's protest was cut short by the capgun *plaap* of the tiny revolver. A vase shattered behind Bolan. He grinned and said, "She's got the drop on us, Phil."

"I'll drop you, too," Andrea angrily told him. "Don't think I can't handle a gun."

"I don't think that," Bolan replied, still grinning.

"Come on, Poppa," Andrea said.

"For God's sake, Andrea, this guy is playing with you. He can shoot both your eyes out before you know he's moving. Get on outta here."

"I said . . ."

"Go on, Deej," Bolan said, cutting Andrea off. "I'm not gunfighting your kid."

DiGeorge said, "That means you get off easy. You get me to running and all you have to do is sit back and laugh and send out your boys to shoot Deej in the back. On some streetcorner. In a car somewhere. I ain't going. We settle this here."

"Don't argue with him, Deej," Marasco pleaded.

Andrea elevated her pistol to shoulder level at full arm-extension, sighting on Bolan. "We leave right now, together, or I start shooting," she warned.

Bolan's .32 was still in his hand. He casually angled it toward DiGeorge. "When I go, Poppa goes," he said simply.

"Deej, get outta here," Marasco urged him.

"I ain't forgetting you, Mr. Philip Honey full of stingers. I ain't forgetting."

"Just go," Bolan said.

DiGeorge went. Andrea went out behind him, the little gun still trained on Bolan. She closed the door and Marasco said, "Well."

"There's still the contract," Bolan philosophized.

"Deej ain't no clown," Marasco said, wetting his lips nervously. "He won't go no further than

174

the first bunch of boys, then he'll be coming back here with 'em."

"I'm not letting him go," Bolan said. He stepped over to the French doors and tugged at the latch. "I didn't want the kid in the middle of this."

"I sure hope there ain't no mistakes about this, Franky," Marasco worried aloud. "I mean, hitting a *Capo* just don't happen every day. Maybe we should check it first. Just to make sure."

"You crazy?" Bolan said. "Who you think you're gonna check with?" He pushed the doors open and stepped onto the lawn. Marasco leapt after him.

"Well, who issues th' contract, Franky?"

"You crazy? Who the hell you think can order a hit on a *Capo*? You gonna ask 'em if maybe they haven't changed their minds? You, Philip Honey?"

"Not me, Franky," Marasco replied quickly.

Bolan fired three rapid shots into the air. Several men whirled and raced toward him. "What's up?" one of them shouted.

"You know Benny Peaceful?" Bolan yelled.

"Hell, yes we know 'im! Is his fingers moving?"

"They damn better get to! I want the gates sealed! Nothin' gets out!"

"Nothin' it is!" the man shouted back. He ran toward the front, two others following. A fourth man stood flat-footed, gawking at Bolan. Bolan raised his .32 and shot him dead where he stood.

"Hey!" Marasco cried. "What's that for?"

Bolan whirled on him with a savage snarl. "Only two kinds are here now. Those that live and those that die. And Benny Peaceful is the line that divides."

"That punk?" Marasco yelled unbelievingly.

"Yeah, it's kind of poetic, isn't it?" Bolan said, suddenly dropping the mask from his Lambretta voice. "Of all the senseless, idiotic killings you lunatics are in for, what could be more senseless and idiotic than letting a Benny Peaceful separate the sheep from the goats?"

"Huh? What?" Marasco was confused and mentally reeling. "I don't get ... what the hell is ... for God's sake! You're Bolan!" He was falling away in shock, clawing for his gun.

"That's right," Bolan said, and put a bullet through the base of his nose. Marasco went over backwards, alarm and betrayal and outrage and fear all evaporating in that final mask of death. "Sorry about that, Philip Honey," Bolan said, actually meaning it, and then he began reloading the .32 and went in search of more game.

Bolan's gun was pre-empted by his own strategy, however. Everyone, by this time, was shooting at everyone. A squad of guards with Thompsons were mowing down everything that moved in the vicinity of the gate. Two vehicles in the parking area were burning. Bodies were strewn about the grounds in various poses of death and near-death. Bolan gave up looking for targets and concentrated on finding Andrea. He did not find the girl outside but he did stumble upon the man who had eluded him on the cliffs of Balboa. Julian DiGeorge lay like a split sandbag with his guts oozing out upon the soil of his kingdom, victim of his own trained assassins and their ever-willing Thompson subs. The big .45 calibre bullets had torn him open, but the *Capo* was still trying to show his dominance of the forces about him, trying to stuff his own entrails back inside with manicured fingers that had not yet received the summons of death. Staring down at him, Bolan was thinking of Doc Brantzen and Genghis Conn and a sweet-faced little lady he had met only in death. He saw the face of pain and surprise on Big Tim Braddock, and he saw the embalmed faces of his own father, mother, and kid sister. He saw the seven grotesque remains of his death squad, and the scores of Mafia dead and dying who had met the Executioner's guns . . . and then he saw only Julian DiGeorge, squirming in the dirt of a kingdom that had not been worth it, and Bolan wondered if anything was worth it. War and violence and death had walked the mountains and valleys of his life for as long as he could remember, and Bolan suddenly could not find any meaningful reasons for any of it. His nose twitched with the smell of death, his ears roared with the screams and moans of the dying, and his eyes smarted with the sight of suffering and torn bodies and blood blood blood everywhere.

Julian DiGeorge looked up at him and said, "Shoot me," in a voice that could not be much longer for this world.

"I wouldn't think of it," Bolan muttered. He stepped away from the dying and went back the way he'd come, across the lawn of death, through the French doors, and into the *Capo's* study.

Andrea D'Agosta was there also, struggling in the grip of one Benny Peaceful, No. 2 Man of Franky Lucky Bolan's new crime empire. Tears were streaming across her cheeks and she screamed out her hate and rage for the man who had brought them there.

Bolan listened to her until her breath ran out, then he said to Benny Peaceful, "You run a sweet hit. Now get on back out there and clean up the garbage. If cops show, and I doubt it, tell 'em Bolan was trying to hit on th' place."

"Sure, Franky," Benny replied. He went to the door, then turned back with an afterthought. "Oh, by the way," he said, "do I move into the villa?"

"Sure," Bolan said wearily. "You take Philip Honey's suite."

Benny Peaceful went out beaming. Bolan stared at the sobbing girl for a moment, then reached for the phone and dialed Carl Lyons.

"I'm glad you called," Lyons said tightly. "I was thinking of trying to contact you. You asked me to check the death of Charles D'Agosta. There's more than a dozen letters from him on file with a congressional committee on organized crime, all of them relating to the financial empire and underworld involvements of Julian DiGeorge. Now Lou Pena was the guy who . . ."

"Hold it," Bolan said tiredly. "Give it to someone who needs it."

He carried the telephone over to Andrea and held the receiver to her ear. "Tell the man to start over," he instructed her.

"Start over," she whispered mechanically. Seconds later she began holding the instrument for herself. Bolan lit a cigarette and smoked while she listened to the policeman's recital. Then she returned the phone to Bolan, said, "Thank you," smoothed her clothing, pushed at her hair, and walked out.

Bolan carried the phone to the desk and sat in DiGeorge's chair. "What's going on out there?" Lyons asked him.

"Just a little house cleaning," Bolan replied, his voice still wearied. "Tell, uh, what's his name—Brognola?—tell him to forget about that portfolio. I've blown it."

"Your cover?" Lyons asked anxiously.

Bolan sighed. "That and everything else. Di-

George is dead and his family is a shambles. They're running around shooting at each other now. I suggest you post a couple of platoons of infantry to watch this place. The fireworks will really start when they all wake up and find out what they've done. Maybe you can pick up a few extra pieces in the process."

The detective whistled to cover an embarrassing loss for words, then murmured, "I don't suppose there's any chance for squaring up your cover. I mean . . ."

"No chance," Bolan tiredly replied. "You can fool some of the fools some of the time, but—no, I'm going to gather up some stuff from Di-George's desk, my final package, and then I'm going to pull a quick fade. Uh, Lyons—thanks, eh."

"Drop the stuff in a locker somewhere and send me the key," Lyons suggested. "Some of us are thanking you, Bolan. But just *some* of us."

"I get the message," Bolan said. He hung up, pulled a briefcase from a bottom drawer of the desk, and began filling it with assorted tidbits from the records of the late Julian DiGeorge. Then he went to the door, took a final look at the Capo's control center, and went out through the familiar corridor.

He found Andrea standing beside the pool, staring dazedly into the water. A fully-clothed body floated there, partially submerged.

"You want to leave with me?" Bolan asked her.

"Where to?" she replied, smiling woodenly.

Bolan shrugged. "Does it matter?" he asked.

She shook her head and placed a hand in his. He led her to the new Mercedes, put her inside, then climbed in and cranked the motor. They spun across to the gate. The man whom Bolan had tagged "Andrew Hardy" glanced at her and showed Bolan a smug grin. A bloodstained handkerchief was wound tightly about one of his hands. He leaned against the Mercedes with his good hand and said, "Quite a show, Franky."

"Yeah," Bolan said. "Tell Benny Peaceful I'm taking care of the kid. Tell 'im I said to watch things until I get back."

"Don't you worry none about Benny," Andrew Hardy reassured him.

Bolan nodded curtly and released the clutch. They cleared the gate with a screech of tires and powered down the lane to the main road. Benny Peaceful did not know it yet, Bolan was thinking, but he needed *everyone's* worry. A family reckoning was coming for *this* day's work. Bolan knew a momentary twinge of sympathy for the insurgents, but clamped it back, seeing the hired guns in their true light: as budding Lou Penas. The world could get along without them.

Andrea looked back briefly as they swung out of the lane. She shuddered, then straightened and moved closer to Bolan. "Whoever you are," she said quietly, "you've just delivered me from purgatory."

Bolan smiled. "There are two ways out of purgatory, you know," he reminded her.

"Which way are we taking?" Andrea murmured.

Bolan could not answer the girl, but he had a pretty good idea of his own route. It would be a familiar one. A shadow life in a shadow world, taking on three dimensions only when someone's blood flowed. Bolan knew ~~his~~ route. He squared his shoulders, encircled her with an arm, and drew her closer. "Just keep looking at that horizon up there," he told her.

"What will that do?" she quietly inquired.

"It will remind you that you're still alive, that

the world is still turning, and that just about anything could happen next."

The girl sighed and moved her head onto his shoulder. They had reached the junction of the main east-west highway. Bolan looked to the west and into the blood-red of a desert sunset. "Oh no," he muttered, swinging east, "I'm not heading into *that*."

But the Executioner did not need a symbolically red sky to overshadow his future. The red of blood was etched into his very shadow, and all compass points would lead inevitably to the same horizon. If there had been reason for the Mafia to hate and fear Mack Bolan in the past, the time was fast approaching when they would rise up with all their wrath and power to crush this greatest of all threats to their continued existence. Pat and Mike lay just across the Executioner's next horizon. In Bolan's shadow world of the immediate future, *all* skies were bloody red.

For the moment, however, there was another victory which was not quite a victory, a good car under him, a straight road ahead, and a warm woman in his arms. Andrea sighed, "Wherever you're heading, just take me with you."

"No hard feelings?" Bolan asked her.

"My Poppa died before I was born, Mack," she said.

"What'd you call me?"

"I'll call you anything you'd like," she whispered.

Bolan sighed through his battle mask. "Just don't call me Lucky," he said, and kissed her, and realized that the mask did not have to be *all* battle.

THE PENETRATOR
by Lionel Derrick

Mark Hardin is a warrior without uniform or rank, pledged to fight anyone on either side of the law who seeks to destroy the American way of life.

Over 1.5 million copies sold!

☐	40-101-2	Target is H	#1	°$1.25
☐	40-102-0	Blood on the Strip	#2	1.25
☐	40-422-0	Capitol Hell	#3	1.50
☐	40-423-9	Hijacking Manhattan	#4	1.50
☐	40-424-7	Mardi Gras Massacre	#5	1.50
☐	40-493-X	Tokyo Purple	#6	1.50
☐	40-494-8	Baja Bandidos	#7	1.50
☐	40-495-6	Northwest Contract	#8	1.50
☐	40-425-5	Dodge City Bombers	#9	1.50
☐	220690-2	Hellbomb Flight	#10	1.25
☐	220728-0	Terror in Taos	#11	1.25
☐	220797-5	Bloody Boston	#12	1.25
☐	40-426-3	Dixie Death Squad	#13	1.50
☐	40-427-1	Mankill Sport	#14	1.50
☐	220882-5	Quebec Connection	#15	1.25
☐	40-456-5	Deepsea Shootout	#16	1.50
☐	40-456-5	Demented Empire	#17	1.50
☐	40-428-X	Countdown to Terror	#18	1.50
☐	40-429-8	Panama Power Play	#19	1.50
☐	40-258-9	Radiation Hit	#20	1.50
☐	40-079-3	Supergun Mission	#21	1.25
☐	40-067-5	High Disaster	#22	1.50
☐	40-085-3	Divine Death	#23	1.50
☐	40-177-9	Cryogenic Nightmare	#24	1.50
☐	40-178-7	Floating Death	#25	1.50
☐	40-179-5	Mexican Brown	#26	1.50